An Offer . . .

The telephone rang, its sharp jangle seeming visibly to jolt the quiet waves of air in the darkened room. Smith lifted the receiver slowly and said, "Hello."

Smith had never before heard the voice, which said, "What kind of deal are you offering?"

"Depends on what you've got," Smith said non-committally. "Suppose you tell me something about yourself."

"What I've got is one of the great stories of our time. A secret agency for the United States government. An official government assassin and his elderly Oriental trainer. A father-son love theme that runs through it. Their battles against evil to try to make America safe for all its people again."

As the voice ranted on, Smith's stomach sank. This man, whoever he was, knew everything. CURE had been compromised.

. . . He Can't Refuse!

THE DESTROYER SERIES FROM PINNACLE

#1 CREATED, THE DESTROYER
#2 DEATH CHECK
#3 CHINESE PUZZLE
#4 MAFIA FIX
#5 DR. QUAKE
#6 DEATH THERAPY
#7 UNION BUST
#8 SUMMIT CHASE
#9 MURDERER'S SHIELD
#10 TERROR SQUAD
#11 KILL OR CURE
#12 SLAVE SAFARI
#13 ACID ROCK
#14 JUDGMENT DAY
#15 MURDER WARD
#16 OIL SLICK
#17 LAST WAR DANCE
#18 FUNNY MONEY
#19 HOLY TERROR
#20 ASSASSIN'S PLAYOFF
#21 DEADLY SEEDS
#22 BRAIN DRAIN
#23 CHILD'S PLAY
#24 KING'S CURSE
#25 SWEET DREAMS
#26 IN ENEMY HANDS
#27 THE LAST TEMPLE
#28 SHIP OF DEATH
#29 THE FINAL DEATH
#30 MUGGER BLOOD
#31 THE HEAD MEN
#32 KILLER CHROMOSOMES
#33 VOODOO DIE
#34 CHAINED REACTION
#35 LAST CALL
#36 POWER PLAY
#37 BOTTOM LINE
#38 BAY CITY BLAST
#39 MISSING LINK
#40 DANGEROUS GAMES
#41 FIRING LINE
#42 TIMBER LINE
#43 MIDNIGHT MAN
#44 BALANCE OF POWER
#45 SPOILS OF WAR
#46 NEXT OF KIN
#47 DYING SPACE
#48 PROFIT MOTIVE
#49 SKIN DEEP
#50 KILLING TIME
#51 SHOCK VALUE
#52 FOOL'S GOLD
#53 TIME TRIAL
#54 LAST DROP
#55 MASTER'S CHALLENGE

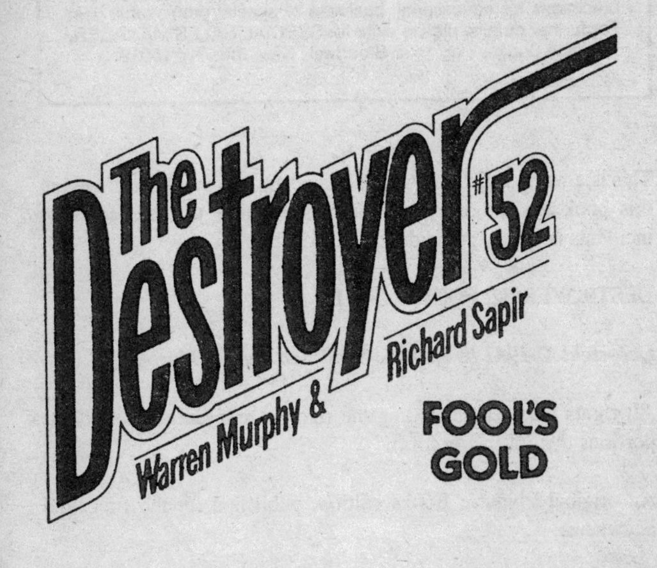

FOOL'S GOLD

PINNACLE BOOKS NEW YORK

DESTROYER 52: FOOL'S GOLD

An original Pinnacle Books edition, published for the first time anywhere.

First printing / May 1983

ISBN: 0-523-41562-1
Can. ISBN: 0-523-43152-X

Cover art by Hector Garrido

Printed in the United States of America

PINNACLE BOOKS, INC.
1430 Broadway
New York, New York 10018

10 9 8 7 6 5 4 3

For Ink. With love.
And for the Glorious House of Sinanju,
P.O. Box 1454, Secaucus, NJ 07094

FOOL'S GOLD

One

She did not expect to see death. She had enough problems with heights. She asked the guide if the ropes were steady, and if he would be steady at the other end.

"Lady," said the guide, "I got hands of steel and a spine of platinum."

"What does a spine of platinum mean?"

"It means don't worry, lady, you ain't gonna fall."

Dr. Terri Pomfret looked up toward the top of the cave. Without a flashlight, she couldn't even see the top of the arched cavern.

Some visiting British spelunkers had crawled up there a month ago while exploring these caves of Albemarle County in North Carolina. They had been going along the ceiling, driving spike after spike, when they came across it. It was a plaque, some kind of metal, chiseled into the stone. They had made a hasty, sloppy rubbing of the stone. No one could identify the writing until it got to Terri Pomfret's office at the university.

"Of course it's Hamidian," she had said.

"Are you sure?"

"Yes. Look at the letters. The formations. Perfect. Perfect ancient Hamidian."

"Then you can read it?"

"This is a bad impression," Terri had said. "I can barely see it."

"If you saw the original, you could read it?"

"Certainly."

"It's at the top of one of the deep Albemarle caves."

"Shit," said Dr. Pomfret.

"Is that negative?" asked her department head.

"What it is is that I hate two things in the world. Going under the ground and going high."

"You're the only one who can do it. And don't worry, Terri, nobody as pretty as you is going to be allowed to fall."

So because of her fear of heights, her guide had strung a rope down from the spikes the British spelunkers had left in the ceiling, and attached a pulley to it. All she would have to do would be to go straight up to the plaque, pulled up by a rope. No climbing along the roof of the cave.

"It's safe, lady," the guide said.

"All right," said Terri. The flashlight was sweaty in her hands and her voice felt weak. Her pencil and paper were strapped to her belt in a little canvas bag. She was 32 years old, with cream-white skin and raven hair and a face that could have been used for a magazine cover, but she preferred to use her mind for her work, not her body.

And now her body was being lifted up to the top of the cave and her breath was stopped as she was thinking, *I will not think about falling to the bottom of the cave. Definitely not. I will not think about falling.*

Falling, she thought. She wondered if the silica sand at the bottom of the cave would soften a fall. The guide's light seemed very far below. She wondered if she released her bladder, what would happen. Then she reminded herself not to breathe.

Then the roof of the cave was up there at her belly and she saw the plaque and she said to herself, "This is not English." And then she said to herself, "Of course not, you beanbag, it's Hamidian. That's why you are here."

The plaque seemed to be chiseled in some rough Hamidian script; as she touched it, she felt that it was metal, but it had been covered with some kind of paint or stain.

She propped her flashlight, like a telephone receiver, between her cheek and shoulder and felt the plaque with both hands. It had the normal Hamidian greeting. It was from one trader to another. Even if she had not seen the markings, she would have suspected Hamidian, because they were the only tribe in the history of South and Central America that had been great traders, and they left themselves messages, such as this one, in many of the spots their ships had visited all over the world. A message at the top of a cave. A message mounted on a stone ceiling 75 feet beneath the ground, discovered only by exact coordinates. That was how they hid their supplies and treasures for each other.

And there they were at the top of the cave, the coordinates. Four inscriptions down and there were guidelines for other Hamidians. She had always been sure the ancient tribe had been to America, too, and here was the proof. She estimated it had occurred several hundred years before Columbus.

But then the Hamidians had died out, apparently killed off by the Spanish when they came to loot the Americas of all their gold. No one had ever found the Hamidian treasures.

She adjusted the flashlight.

A mountain? They were storing a mountain? Why would the Hamidians store a mountain? Why would they want to protect a mountain?

She got the next word. It was confusing. It meant valuable. It could also mean coin in some contexts. It was a very common word for the Hamidians. Would they exaggerate? In poetry, yes. In a message to their fellow Hamidian traders, no. They were very literal and precise.

Therefore, there was an entire mountain made of coins, thought Terri. Her back hurt. She wondered why her back hurt. Oh, yes. She was hoisted up here at the top of the cave and the rope was biting into her back.

Mountain of coins. She remembered one of the first Hamidian poems she had ever translated. That word was in it. A mountain of pure coins. The sun glowed like a mountain of pure coins.

No. The sun glowed like a mountain of gold. Gold. An entire mountain of pure gold.

And she was falling.

"You damned idiot," she screamed. "Hold that rope. I'm getting the coordinates."

The rope jumped again and she kicked, feeling a sway, seeing the plaque go farther away from her before she had the coordinates. She was swinging and the coordinates were up there getting farther and farther away and then she realized the rope was sinking through the piton and she was swinging wide like a pendulum, falling, in longer and longer arcs.

She felt her back would break where the rope held her, the flashlight went flying, the notepad went flying, and then she hit a wall at the far end of a swing. But it was not a hard hit, more like being bumped by a big man. It must have been at the outer reach of the arc, just before she came back. And she bumped again, and at the lowest point of the arc she brushed the ground with her legs, and that diminished the force of her fall, leaving her in the soft silica dust with the coils of rope coming down after her.

It took a few moments to get her breath. She felt her legs and her arms. No severe pain. Nothing was broken. A sharp yellow light about fifty feet from her illuminated a patch on the cave wall. The guide had not only dropped her, he had dropped his flashlight.

"Butterfingers," she said angrily. "Idiot, goddam butterfingers." He didn't answer. She had to get up herself and walk over to the flashlight herself and pick up the flashlight herself and then look around for the butterfingered moron.

The flashlight was warm and moist and sticky. She couldn't see what the liquid was and she didn't really care to. She wanted to find the butterfingered clown who had let her drop. She shone the flashlight around the cave.

"Shmuck," she said. "All right. Have you run

away? Is that what you did, butterfingers?" She was almost crying, she was so angry. How could he do this to her? Him and his spine of platinum. Really.

She felt something beneath her foot in the soft silica sand, something like a small tube. Had butterfingers dropped that too?

She pointed the flashlight at the ground. And then she realized why her guide had butterfingers. She was looking at them. His fingers had all been cut off. And so had an arm, and the head was looking at her with that stupid open-pupiled gaze of the dead.

Dr. Terri Pomfret, professor of ancient languages, let out a scream in the Albemarle Caves that didn't stop until she realized that there was no one around to hear her. Unless, of course, it was the person who had done this to her guide.

Whoever it was did not come after her. And she made it outside, after what seemed like almost a full day of dazed wandering. It had been forty minutes, and the sticky liquid on the flashlight was blood.

She would have bet at that moment that the last place she would ever return would be to that cave. The police could find no suspect. Indeed, for a while, she was the suspected murderer of the guide, but then the investigation just died out, and one day soon after several men visited her. They were from the government and they asked her if she loved her country.

"Yes. I guess. Of course," she said.

"Then I think you ought to know what a mountain of gold is," said one of the men.

"It's a load of gold," said Terri.

"No, no. That's what a truckload of gold is. A mountain of gold," he said solemnly, "is the most dangerous strategic asset any nation can have. It is pure wealth. It isn't like oil that is vulnerable and in the ground. It is the most liquid wealth anyone could have. In such quantity, whoever owned it could literally control the world."

Terri couldn't believe it. Here she was talking to the government and they were talking nonsense at her.

"Do you really believe the mountain exists?" Terri asked. "I mean, even if the Hamidians were very specific when they were writing about money, well, let's face it, a mountain of gold is . . . well, a mountain of gold. I just don't think there is that much in the world."

Dr. Pomfret did not understand, said the men from the government. The possibility that the mountain might exist was so dangerous that they had to go looking for it.

Quietly, the government had called in geologists and mineral experts and they theorized about the structure of the earth and mining capabilities over the years, and on and on, and they said, yes, maybe there could be a mountain of gold.

"I'm not going to go back into that cave," Terri said.

"Meet Bruno," said the men from the government. Bruno was six-feet-five and had a head shaved like a bullet and a neck like heavy plumbing for an aircraft carrier. His hands were as wide as a breadbox. Hair grew on his fingertips.

Bruno smiled a lot. He picked up a telephone in Dr. Pomfret's office and squeezed it until the wiring popped out like carnival-colored spaghetti.

"This is your bodyguard, Dr. Pomfret."

Bruno's voice was surprisingly cultured, with even a bit of arrogance in it.

"I have never lost a client yet, Dr. Pomfret."

"I can see," she said.

"You can trust me," said Bruno.

"Yes. Well, all right," said Terri. He was big and he was strong and he did give that feeling of assurance. She was up and down in the cave that afternoon, with the entire inscription translated and the coordinates accurate.

Outside the cave, Bruno kept telling her how he never lost anyone. His grin became bigger. He told her how most assassins and killers were dumb. That the guide had to be especially stupid to get his head cut off like that. And his fingers and his arms.

Bruno assumed that the killer had apparently seen him and exercised some rare intelligence.

"He's probably running right now, back where he came from," said Bruno as they entered his little M.G. convertible. Bruno smiled again. Bruno put the key into the ignition. Bruno smiled again. Bruno turned the key in the ignition. Bruno's head fell off into Terri Pomfret's lap.

She was looking at a gushing severed neck and the head was in her lap. This time when she screamed, not even her sore throat could stop the yelling. People had to lift her out of the car still screaming. She was under sedation for a week.

When the doctors said she could talk, a government representative came into her room. Terri felt as if she were on a cloud and she was also feeling that when she got off the cloud, the terror would begin again.

The government official was apologetic.

"Well, golly, I guess we did it again, didn't we?" he said. "Seriously, however——"

"Uhhh," said Terri and slipped into comfortable blackness. The doctors explained to the government man that even though the hospital could give the patient sedation, she also had her own form of self-sedation that mankind had used throughout history.

"What's that?" the government man asked.

"It's called passing out in terror," said the doctor.

"Was it a loud scream? Was her whole body in it? Did her breasts move when she screamed?"

Neville Lord Wissex waited for an answer. He wanted to know exactly. He sat in the great hall of Wissex Castle, in afternoon grays, with a magnum of new Peruvian white, that made most Chablis taste like a soft drink. A subtle dash of cocaine always aroused the true bouquet of a white wine.

Outside the window, the British countryside rolled in a pleasant and rare sunny day, green hill to green hill, the ancient estate of the Wissexes. Behind Lord Wissex were stuffed heads, mounted on mahogany, with small brass plates under the necks. The eyes looked realistic because they came from ocular prosthodontics. People used glass eyes for moose. Why use less for humans?

The Wissex family always insisted that the eyes be the same color as the subject. Therefore, the head of Lord Mulburry had green eyes as he had had in life. And Field Marshal Roskovsky had blue and General Maximilian Garcia y Gonzales y Mendosa y Aldomar Bunch had deep brown eyes. As they had had in life.

But the heads were old. The House of Wissex did not take heads any more. One did not need them as a selling point anymore. Not in this rich world market made so bountiful by all the new countries created after World War II.

Wissex wanted to hear exactly how the woman screamed and after the Gurkha knifeman explained how he had made sure the head fell into the lap by the angle of the cut as Lord Wissex had suggested and how the woman could not control herself, Lord Wissex smiled and said it was time to dispense with pleasure and get down to business.

A small computer terminal rested on a silver tray. Wissex punched the result of the job into the computer. There were certain things one did not let servants do. One had to do these things oneself if one wanted to continue to prosper.

"Let me see your thrust again if you would be so kind," said Wissex.

The Gurkha made the short smooth thrust and Wissex punched its description into the computer.

"Yes, that's fine," Wissex said, calling in a draw from the computer. It showed immediately how many knife fighters were in the employ of the House of Wissex, how many could be recruited, how many could be trained in how much time and the general state of the market at the moment. They had lost some people in a small job in Belgium that the local authorities there had mistaken for a sex attack because the victim happened to be a woman and the weapons used were knives.

But there would be no more jobs like that if this new one worked. The House of Wissex would be able to go on for the next ten years on just this job if it worked.

Lord Wissex looked at the market pattern on the screen with wedges going to the Middle East, to South America and Africa. There was so much good business in the Third World nowadays, but this one could put them all to shame.

"We're going to promote you and give you a raise," said Wissex, looking up at the Gurkha. They might need many good knife fighters soon, if everything worked out as beautifully as it had in the caves of North Carolina.

When Terri recovered, she thought she heard a government man say she was going to be protected by a force so great and so secret that even the head of the department only knew that the President had given such assurance.

"The President of the United States, Terri, is personally authorizing a protection so awesome we don't even know what he's talking about. How is that?"

"How is what?" said Terri. She was fighting with all her strength to keep some broth down in her stomach.

"You are going to be protected by something only the President can authorize."

"Protected for what?" Terri Pomfret asked.

"You're going back into that cave," said the man.

Terri thought that was what he said. She could have sworn that was what he said. But she wasn't quite sure, however, because she was in a very comfortable, deep blackness.

Two

His name was Remo and the sun was setting red over Bay Rouge in St. Maarten as he guided his sloop to a slow anchor in the small bay.

The West Indies island was the size of a county back in the states, but it was a perfect location to beam and receive information from satellite traffic in space. That was what he had been told.

The island was half French and half Dutch and therefore, in that confusion, America could do just about anything without being suspected. It was the perfect island for a special project, except that it had too many people.

Seventeen too many.

Jean Baptiste Malaise and his sixteen brothers lived in grand houses between Marigot and Grand Case, two villages that were barely large enough to deserve that name, but which had more fine restaurants than almost any American city, and all of Britain, Asia, and Africa. Combined.

Fine yachts would dock at Marigot or Grand Case for their owners to enjoy the cuisine. And sometimes, if the owners were alone and returned to their yachts alone, sometimes they were never seen again and their boats, under a different name and different flag, would join the drug fleet of the Malaise family.

The family might never have been bothered except that the island had to be clean. And it had to be cleaned of seventeen people too many. There could be no outside force functioning on the island.

The initial plan was that Remo would purchase a powerboat, just the kind that the Malaise were known to prefer for their drug traffic—two Chrysler engines with a specific gear-to-power ratio, a certain kind of propellor, a certain kind of cabin, a special decking that they absolutely loved, and a rakish swept configuration that was produced largely by a California man in conjunction with a Florida motor assembly works.

Remo would take this boat and dock on the eastern side of the island. Then he would go to a restaurant alone, allow himself to be followed by one of the seventeen Malaise brothers, and then quietly dispose of him somewhere off the island.

He would continue to do this until the remaining brothers stopped following him, and then he would quietly remove whoever was left.

But the plan didn't work. The problem was the boat. He had bought the right boat in St. Bart's, a neighboring island, right on time a month ago.

But the boat needed what Remo understood was a "fuesal." Everybody else he brought the boat to didn't know what a fuesal was. When someone finally figured out he was mispronouncing the item, three weeks of his time had gone and no one could get the part for another month because it had to be flown in from Denmark.

He never did find out what a fuesal was exactly. He pointed to another boat.

"Give me that," he had said.

"That is not a powerboat, sir."

"Does it run?"

"Yes. On sail with an auxiliary motor."

"Sails I don't need. Does the motor run and does it have enough gas to get me to St. Maarten?"

"Yes. I imagine so."

"I want it," Remo said.

"You want the sloop," the man said.

"I want the thing that has enough gas to get me from here," said Remo, pointing to his feet, "to there." He pointed to the large volcanic island of St. Maarten, squatting under the Caribbean sun.

So instead of a powerboat a month earlier, a powerboat that the Malaise family would have coveted, he had a sloop and now he had only 24 hours to clean the island.

He made it to St. Martin easily in the unfamiliar boat because he did not have to turn too much.

He was a thin man and he slipped into the water of Bay Rouge without a wrinkle on a wave. No one on the beach noticed that his arms did not flail the water like most swimmers, but that that body moved by the exact and powerful thrusts of the spinal column, pushing it forward, more like a shark than a man.

The arms merely guided everything. There was hardly any wake behind the swimmer and then he went underwater so silently one could have watched him, and thought only, "Did I really see a man swimming out there?"

He moved up out of the water onto a rocky part of the shore with the speed of a chameleon, like man's first ascent from the sea. He was thin and without visible musculature. His clothes clung wet and sticky to his body but he allowed the heat to escape from his pores and as he walked in the evening air, the clothing became dry.

The first person he met, a little boy, knew where the Malaises lived. The boy spoke in the singsong of the West Indies.

"They are all along the beach here, good sir, but I would not go there without permission. No one goes there. They have wire fences that shock. They have the alligator in the pools around their houses. No one visits the Malaise, good sir, unless of course they invite you."

"Pretty bad people, I guess," said Remo.

"Oh, no. They buy things from everyone. They are nice," the boy said.

The electric fence was little more than a few wide strands that might keep an arthritic old cow from trying to dance out of its field. The moat with alligators was a moist marsh area with an old alligator too well fed to do anything but burp softly as Remo passed its jaws. Remo could see the house had small holes in the walls for gunbarrels. But there were also air conditioners in the windows, and nothing appeared to be locked. Obviously the Malaises no longer feared anyone or anything.

Remo knocked on the door of the house and a

tired woman, still beating a food mixture in a bowl, answered the door.

"Is this the home of Jean Malaise?"

The woman nodded. She called out something in French and a man answered gruffly from inside the house.

"What do you want?" asked the woman.

"I've come to kill him and his brothers."

"You don't have a chance," said the woman. "They have guns and knives. Go back and get help before you try."

"No, no. That's all right," Remo said. "I can do it by myself."

"What does he want?" called the man's voice in heavily accented English.

"Nothing, dear. He is going to come back later."

"Tell him to bring some beer," yelled her husband.

"I don't need help," Remo told the woman.

"You're just one man. I have lived with Jean Baptiste for twenty years. I know him. He is my husband. Will you at least listen to a wife? You don't stand a chance against him alone, let alone the entire clan."

"Don't tell me my business," Remo said.

"You come here. You come to our island. You knock on the door and when I try to tell you you don't know my husband, you say it is your business. Well, I tell you, good. Then die."

"I'm not going to die," said Remo.

"Hah," said the wife.

"Is he going to bring back beer?" called the husband.

"No," said the wife.

"Why not?"

"Because he is one of those Americans who think they know everything."

"I don't know everything," Remo said. "I don't know what a fuesal is."

"For a boat?"

Remo nodded.

"Jean knows," said the woman, and then, full-lung: "Jean, what is a fuesal?"

"What?"

"A fuesal?"

"Never heard of it," the man called back.

Remo went into the main room where Jean Baptiste, a large man with much girth and much hair on that girth, sat on a straight-backed chair. His hair glistened with oil. He had shaved no sooner than a week before. He belched loudly.

"I don't know what a fuesal is," he said. He was watching television; Remo saw Columbo in French. It seemed funny to have the American talk in loud and violent French.

"It's better in English," Remo said.

Jean Baptiste Malaise grunted.

"Listen, Mr. Malaise, I've come to kill you and all your brothers."

"I'm not buying anything," said Malaise.

"No. I said kill."

"Wait until the commercial."

"I don't really have much time."

"All right. What? What do you want?" said Malaise, his black eyes burning with anger. This was his favorite television show.

"I have come," said Remo, very slowly and very clearly, "to kill you and your sixteen brothers."

"Why is that?"

"Because we cannot have another armed force on the island."

"Who is this we?"

"It's a secret organization. I can't tell you about it."

"What secret organization?"

"I said I can't talk about it," Remo said.

"It's a game."

"Not a game. You and your brothers are going to be dead by morning."

"Do I sign something? When do I get the prize?" asked Malaise.

"I have come here to kill you and your brothers and you will all be dead before tomorrow noon," said Remo.

"All right. What for?" said Jean Malaise. The commercial was on now and he didn't like commercials.

"Because you murder people on their boats and smuggle drugs into America with those boats."

"So why kill me? We've always done that. Are we cutting into your market?"

"Listen," said Remo, feeling a rare sense of anger. "I am not here because I am a competitor. I am here because you are going to die. Tonight. And your sixteen brothers."

"Shhhh, the commercial's over."

"Mrs. Malaise," said Remo. "Would you please call all the brothers here? I want to see them tonight."

"They were here last night," said Mrs. Malaise.

"Just call them and tell them to bring weapons if they want."

"They always carry weapons."

"Call them," Remo said.

"They are really going to kill you," said the woman.

"Call," said Remo and then to Jean Malaise, "What's happening? I don't understand French."

"This detective, Mr. Columbo, who is French on his mother's side, is outsmarting the British."

"I think they've changed the story line in translation," Remo said. "You wouldn't happen to know what a fuesal is?"

"That again?" said Malaise.

"It goes on a boat and is about eight inches long and has ball bearings and does something with the fuel mixture or something."

"No," said Malaise, still absorbed by the picture.

"You doing a good business?" Remo asked.

"It's a living," the man said.

"So far," said Remo.

It took the brothers less than 20 minutes to assemble in the living room. Remo could not remember their names. He waited until Columbo was over and then spoke to all of them.

"Quiet. Will you please? Quiet. *Quiet*. Shhh. Will you listen? I've come here to kill you. Now we can do it here, but I suggest outside because the floors here will get messy as hell."

"What is the game?" said one.

"There's no game," Remo said.

"Jean Baptiste says you are giving away something for a game show. We will be on American television."

"No, no. You will not be on American television. You are all going to die tonight because I am going to kill you. All right, is that clear?"

There was much confused talking in French and there were a few angry voices. They all looked to the oldest brother, Jean Baptiste Malaise.

"Okay, you sonofabitch, now you going to die. You come here interrupting Columbo and bringing no beer and then lying about us being on television. You will die. We've killed hundreds."

"Not in my living room," screamed Mrs. Malaise.

"Outside," said Malaise.

"Not in the peonies," said Mrs. Malaise.

Remo was the last one outside and Jean Baptiste tried a simple turn with a pistol. It was basically just hiding the pistol, then turning and firing straight ahead on the turn, but Remo caught the wrist before its fingers could fire and smoothly pushed the sternum up into the heart, stopping it. He caught three temples immediately, stopping the brains, and followed the others who had yet to turn around with six blows, rapid, using both hands, sending fragments of the occipital into the brain, three strokes, two hands, one, two, three, very rapidly like an automatic riveter. Two others were turning around with knives as he caught their skulls at the coronal sutures, splitting the casing of the brains and rupturing them.

One of the brothers had a submachine gun and was waiting to get a shot. He waited forever. He couldn't quite pull the trigger because his arm had been crushed at the elbow. He didn't even see the hand go through the suborbital notch of the skull. There was just darkness.

Another was squeezing off a shot from a .357

magnum with which he had personally taken 22 lives in desperate island coves. He could have sworn he was pointing the gun at the stranger but if that were so, why was he looking at the flash? He did not look long. The big shell exploded in his face.

Another had a length of chain with a heavy copper-pointed lead slug at the end that he cracked bottles with for practice and faces with for real. Somehow the stranger caught this deadly slug being whipped with centrifugal force with one delicate finger and just as delicately put it back into the face that had seen so many others die.

And then there were two, the last two pirates of St. Maarten.

One emptied the clip of a 9-mm pistol at the stranger. He could have sworn he was hitting the body but the body did not drop. It was dark that night with only a sliver of moonlight. It became much darker very quickly and forever.

And then there was one. He had intended to finish off whatever there was to finish off, but no one ever left him with much in the way of combat. It had been his job to kill the children left over on boats stranded in the Caribbean and he liked the work because he was the cruelest.

"Leave something for me," he called, turning around, and then he saw that it was all left for him. "Oh," he said.

"Yes," said the stranger.

So the last Malaise looked at his sixteen dead brothers and knew it was up to him. Well, he was the most cunning Malaise. He was the one who had trained his body to perfection. He was the Malaise who held not only the black belt in karate but the famed red belt. He had blended karate with taekwondo.

He had never needed weapons.

He went into his battle position and assumed the posture of the cobra, hissing the power into every sinew of his body.

The stranger chuckled. "What's that?"

"Find out."

"Don't have time for the play stuff," the American said.

The last Malaise saw the stranger's skull and prepared the blow that could not even be seen by human eyes, such was its speed. It came from the very bottom of his feet and went out at the stranger's frontal lobe, driving, striking . . . unfortunately, without much power because the body was not behind it. The body was not behind it because the arm was going forward and the body was going backward, and the last Malaise was dead.

"Leave them there," said Mrs. Malaise.

"I was going to clean them up," Remo said.

"Don't bother. We're going to have funerals so the undertaker can do it. Have you eaten?"

"Yeah. I'm not hungry. I've got to find a place here and do something else by noon tomorrow."

"You're kind of cute. Spend the night. You don't want to go walking around the island at night."

"I've got to."

"Part of the quiz game?" the woman asked.

"Sure," lied Remo.

"What do I get for telling you what a fuesal is?"

"Nothing," Remo said.

"It's a form of Balinese makeup."

"Wrong," said Remo. "It's got something to do with boats."

"Right. What was I thinking of? Is there a consolation prize?"

"You have the funerals. You get all their money if you're smart," Remo said. "What more do you want?"

"Never hurts to ask," said Mrs. Malaise. Remo walked out beyond the sleepy alligator and the loose strands of electrical wire and back to the main road, a narrow two-lane and nothing to spare strip that surrounded the island.

On this island, Upstairs could create all the traffic it wanted and it would blend with the tourists who kept the restaurants filled. Upstairs could do all its international work in serving America, as the powerful secret organization that did not exist on paper. It could never be exposed to light or investigated by some headline-hungry politician because it simply never was.

And now its foreign operations were moving to this ideal island. As Upstairs had said, in the form of one rather dry, Dr. Harold W. Smith, director: "It is a perfect base for satellite communication. It is easy to disguise ingress and egress among the tourists. And best of all, it is not American soil. If our cover gets blown, at worst it can be blamed on the CIA."

And since the key to the operations was the vast and complex computer system that monitored key financial and criminal traffic in the world, Smith had an even better plan. A far safer plan than any physical transfer of the records of international violence and crime.

The records would be lost if they were physically carried from one spot to another. But they would be absolutely safe if they were beamed in code from one computer system to another, from the home base in Rye, New York, where the organization's cover identity, Folcroft Sanitarium, was located, to the new one on St. Maarten Island.

As Smith had explained, since human hands would not touch it, since no tangible object would carry it, since it would happen in microseconds, the crucial information that the organization ran on would be safer in transit by satellite beam than any other way. Just as safe as if the information remained in headquarters in America—safer even, because America with all its probing groups and publicity-happy politicians could become a bit uncomfortable. There had been too many close calls, Smith told Remo. Too many people that Remo had had to quiet forever.

Remo had said, "Not that many. You ought to leave things where they are."

And Smith had said it was better to beam the records to St. Martin, and Remo had said, "If it ain't broke, don't fix it," but Smith hadn't listened.

Remo walked past the small villages, hearing frogs croak in marshland ponds, through streets so narrow they could not accommodate two passing cars and a pedestrian side by side, past elegant restaurants and then he turned right.

A small airstrip was to his right with a building the size of a woodshed. An innocuous little private airfield.

Behind it stood a neat new building with the sign, Analogue Networking, Inc., the new high-tech business of St. Maarten. Smith had explained that they would employ at least one hundred people off the island without one of them understanding what he was being paid to do. Which was crucial for the cover. All operatives of CURE, the secret organization, did not know what they were doing or who they were working for. Except Smith and Remo. And Remo didn't care.

Remo introduced himself at the Analogue Networking gate and forgot the password. It was not unusual for high-tech industries to have passwords lest someone steal valuable microchips.

Remo suggested "Tippecanoe and Tyler Too."

"It's 'Mickey Mouse,' " the guard said. Then he shrugged. "You close enough. One can't be too much the stickler, can one?"

"Nope," said Remo agreeably.

Remo waited inside the plant until morning when the programmer arrived with a large loaf of fresh French bread, less than an hour from the bakery ovens. Remo refused a bite. He had eaten only two days before and his body wouldn't need anything for a few days more. Still, the smell was good and reminded him of the days when he ate normally, before his training, before so many things.

Five minutes before noon, he saw the technician punch instructions into a machine. The technician explained that the computers operated the radio aerial outside so as to get the best and clearest lock on the overhead satellite. No human hands would touch it.

A phone call came on a private line, not attached to the island's telephone communications.

It was Smith for Remo.

"We're going to be sending in a minute. You understand what that means? Nothing will be here. Everything will be there once the transmission is complete. We are erasing completely here."

"I don't understand that stuff, Smitty."

"You don't have to. Just stay on the phone."

"Not going anywhere," Remo said, looking at the technician in front of the computer console. The technician smiled. Remo smiled. More than a dozen years of secret investigations would be moved any moment through space to the discs in this computer. The technician only knew he was getting records; he didn't know what records, and if he had learned, it would have meant his life.

There was a crackle on the telephone line with Smith. Probably some storm across the thousands of miles of open sea.

"Okay," said Smith.

"What?" said Remo.

"Done," said Smith. "What's your reading down there?"

"What's our reading?" Remo asked the technician.

"Ready when he is," said the technician.

"Ready when you are, Smitty," Remo said.

"They are already gone," Smith said.

"He says he sent them," Remo told the technician.

The technician shrugged. "Nothing here."

"Nothing here," Remo said.

"But I got an acknowledgement," said Smith.

"We send an acknowledgement?" asked Remo. The technician shook his head. "Not from us, Smitty," Remo said.

"Oh, no," groaned Smith. Remo thought that it might just have been the first emotion he had ever heard wrung from the tight-lipped CURE director. "Someone has our records and we don't know who."

"Want anything else?" Remo asked pleasantly.

"There may not be anything else," Smith said.

"I don't trust machinery," Remo said, and he hung up and headed toward where he knew Smith could reach him if he wanted.

Barry Schweid was looking for the new gimmick, the totally new concept that would catapult him from the dinky $200,000 screenplay to the $500,000 plus gross. To do that, his agent said, he had to be original.

No copying *Star Wars* or *Raiders of the Lost Ark* or *Jaws*.

"Copy something nobody else is copying."

"Everybody is copying everything," Schweid said.

"Copy something new," said the agent, so Barry had a brilliant idea. He had all the old scripts put on computers, really old scripts. He would blend all the great old ideas, even from the old silent flicks. But in the middle of creating a new script, he panicked. Copying the oldies was just too original for him. He had to hook into newer material. So he had a disc satellite antenna put up outside his Hollywood home. He had the disc arranged to pick up all the new television shows and transform them by sound into scripts.

But on the first day, the whole computer system went crazy. There was no script. The software used up his entire supply of storage material which he had been assured could not be used up in a hundred years.

And then when he went to address his newest script to the producers, Bindle and Marmelstein, he saw the strangest readout. It was no package label that came out of the machine but three full sheets of computer readout, as to the strange ways Bindle and Marmelstein financed pictures.

They were connected with the biggest cocaine dealer in Los Angeles. And there it all was on the computer printouts. How much the man dealt, where his home was, who were his sources of drugs in South America, how Bindle and Marmelstein helped move the coke through the film industry.

There were many strange things on the computer and Schweid hadn't ordered any of them. He called the computer supplier.

"There was a storm over the Atlantic the other day. Fouled up receptions from all the satellite stations," said the supplier.

"So if I got some information, it wouldn't necessarily be wrong, but it might just be information I wasn't supposed to have gotten," Schweid said.

"Yeah, I guess so. It was all scrambled, all over the atmosphere."

When Barry confronted Hank Bindle and Bruce Marmelstein, the producers, and told them he knew about their cocaine connection, they promised that Barry would never again sell a script in the business, that this was an outrage, that he had sunk lower than anyone else in Hollywood had ever sunk before. Bruce Marmelstein's indignation was such that Hank Bindle fell into tears, realizing the depth of hurt in his partner.

Both of them were in tears when Bruce finished talking about freedom of information meaning freedom for all mankind. That done, Bruce asked Barry Schweid what he wanted them to give him to keep quiet.

"I want to do *Hamlet.*"

"*Hamlet,*" said Bruce. He handled the business affairs of the company. He had a wide Valium smile. "What's *Hamlet*?"

"It's old stuff. It's British, I think," said Hank Bindle. He was the creative arm of the production team. He dressed in sneakers and tennis shirts and looked like Bo Peep but those who knew him had the sense that he was more like the contents of a sewage system. But without the richness.

"James Bond, you're talking," said Bruce.

"No," said Barry. "It's a great play. It's by Shakespeare, I think."

"Naaaah. No box office," said Marmelstein.

"Let's see how much coke you fellows moved last year," said Barry.

"Okay. *Hamlet*. But with tits. We got to have tits," said Marmelstein.

"There were no tits in Hamlet," Barry said.

"All men? Gay?" said Hank Bindle.

"No," said the writer. "There was Ophelia."

"We'll have Ophelia with the biggest set of tits since Genghis Khan," said Bruce.

"Genghis Khan was a man," Barry Schweid said.

"With a name like Genghis? A man?" said Bruce, shocked. He looked at Hank Bindle. "I think so," Bindle said. As the creative arm, he was supposed to be able to read newspapers and everything, even ones without pictures.

"Was this Genghis Khan gay?" asked Marmelstein.

"No," Schweid said. "He was a great Mongol conqueror."

"I never heard of a mongrel with a name like Khan," said Marmelstein. "He was probably gay."

When Remo arrived at the condominium, set above the blue waters of Miami Beach, he brought a duck and some rice for the following day's dinner.

A wisp of a man with delicate strands of white beard and white locks coming down over his ears sat on the veranda. He wore a kimono and did not turn to answer when Remo called his name.

"Little Father," Remo said again. "Is everything all right?"

Chiun, the Master of Sinanju, said nothing.

Remo did not know if Chiun was being quiet or if he was just ignoring Remo. There was no way that he had not heard him. Chiun could hear an elevator start on the next block.

"I got the duck," Remo said.

"Yes, of course, the duck," Chiun said. Right. It was ignoring that he was doing.

"Is something wrong?" Remo asked.

"What should be wrong? I'm used to this."

"Used to what, Little Father?"

"I said I was used to it."

Chiun looked out to the sea, his long fingernails folded into each other.

Remo thought, *I will not ask. He wants me to ask.* Remo started the slow boiling of the rice. He looked back at Chiun and surrendered.

"All right. What are you used to?" he asked.

"I am so used to it I hardly notice."

"You notice enough to ignore me," Remo said.

"Some things one cannot shut out, no matter how hard he tries."

"What?"

"Did you enjoy St. Maarten?" Chiun asked.

"You didn't want to go. I had to take seventeen brothers all at once by myself. I could have used you. Fortunately, they bunched up so there wasn't any problem. But you know seventeen is seventeen."

"Has it come to this?" Chiun asked woefully.

"What?"

"You're trying to use guilt on your teacher. On the trainer who has given you the awesome power of Sinanju. And now guilt? Guilt for what? For giving you what no white man has ever had? Giving from my own blood and breathing. And then you come here after being gone for a month and you try to make me feel guilty?"

"What did I do?" Remo asked.

"Nothing," said Chiun and turned to the window in silence.

In Miami Beach the next day, the telephone rang. The call was for Remo. Smith would be coming into Miami. Apparently there was something even more important than CURE's lost files.

Had Remo or Chiun, in their travels, ever heard of a mountain of gold?

Three

The knife went into the throat perfectly, slicing across the jugular and cutting the windpipe, rendering the soldier helpless.

Neville Lord Wissex stepped back so that Generalissimo Moombasa Garcia y Benitez could see his soldier die, could see how well the knife fighter worked.

"We take a regular Gurkha soldier and give him further training, as you can see," said Lord Wissex. He wore a pinstriped business suit with vest and gray leather gloves.

The generalissimo watched. He could have sworn his soldier would have killed the knife fighter, for the soldier had the very effective street club that all the generalissimo's soldiers carried when they helped protect the liberated people of modern Hamidia.

Hamidia was bounded by three Latin-American countries that would have had the most repressive regimes in South America if it were not for Generalissimo Moombasa's.

Two things, however, saved Moombasa from

protests by the world. From without and within. One, his soldiers with clubs would kill protesters very often and very thoroughly. That took care of protest from within. Second, he had wisely put a hammer and sickle on his flag, called his country the "People's Democratic Republic of Hamidia" and went about talking socialism as piles of people, who were foolish enough to whisper unkind things about him, went up in flames. Moombasa called them "my bonfires." The world outside Hamidia ignored the bonfires and concentrated only on the hammer and sickle. No protests from there either.

Once, when he got tired of burning people, he tried to take over Uruguay, Paraguay, and Venezuela. He did this by killing bathers, schoolchildren, bus drivers, airplane passengers, people in restaurants, and any other unprotected citizens with his soldiers, who were generally too cowardly to fight other soldiers.

Attacks on civilians were not considered atrocities because Moombasa called them "battles in the war of liberation." Promptly, three quarters of the newspapers in Great Britain and half its universities opened their minds to his far-reaching philosophies.

At first he had said, "I don't got no philosophy. I kill people."

But it was then that he and Neville Lord Wissex became fast and true friends. He called Lord Wissex "my good friend Neville."

Of course, half the other people he had called his good friends were now charred remnants buried on the outskirts of Liberation City, his capital. The other half killed for him.

Wissex had said to him: "We'll get you a philosophy and then you can kill anyone you want in any way you want and you will be respected in the world community. Nothing you can do will be condemned except by people you can call names yourself."

"What kind of philosophy?" Moombasa had asked. He thought it might have something to do with not eating meat.

"Marxism. Just say you are the people and anyone against you is against the people and therefore you are defending the people as you kill anyone you want. But you must always blame everything that goes wrong on the United States of America. And sometimes Great Britain."

Moombasa couldn't believe how well it worked. He spent municipal taxes on a new pleasure boat for himself instead of sewage disposal and half a city died from the ensuing diseases. Then he blamed American imperialism for the suffering of his people, and immediately scores of new articles appeared in Europe and America describing how the generalissimo fought hunger, disease, and American imperialism.

It gave him an international license to kill. Having been granted that, he made his first important purchase from Lord Wissex: a delayed-action bomb and, more importantly, the Wissex employees to deliver it.

He almost toppled two neighboring governments that way, before they sent armies to his borders, and he suddenly decided they were brothers in the never-ending battle against American aggression and tyranny.

But now, Lord Wissex was asking an astounding price for knife fighters.

"Five million dollars?" said Moombasa. "Let me see the knife."

Lord Wissex nodded the Gurkha knifeman to approach the large chair on which the generalissimo sat. The Gurkha handed the blade hilt forward.

Moombasa looked at the knife. He felt the blade. It was sharp. He ran a hand across the back of the blade. It was curved.

"I give you twenty-five dollars," said the generalissimo to Wissex.

Lord Wissex smiled tolerantly.

"That's ten dollars too much, my friend Moombasa, President for Life. It is not the knife. It's the delivery. You can buy a lump of lead for a penny, but delivered from a high-powered special sniper's rifle, that bullet costs much more. It is not the material but what you want to do with it that costs," Wissex said.

"Right. I got no one worth five million dollars dead," said the generalissimo, handing back the knife. He told the Gurkha who had killed his soldier, "Nice cut, kiddo."

"You don't want to kill someone, old friend," said Lord Wissex. "You want to capture someone."

"I don't want to torture no one worth five million."

"You probably won't have to torture her," said Wissex.

"Her? I can get any woman I want in Hamidia for ten bucks, two thousand in Hamidian cash, which is——"

"Nine ninety-five today," whispered an aide who

had one of the few secure jobs in the nation. He could read and count. Sometimes without moving his lips. "The exchange rate down again today."

"Right," said the generalissimo. "Nine ninety-five."

"You want to talk to her," Wissex said.

"Ain't nobody I want to talk to five million dollars worth."

"Ah, but you do. Talk to her and you may become the richest, most powerful man in the world."

"God is good," said Moombasa. "How?"

"The ancient Hamidians that first settled this land were the greatest traders of the ancient world. They created a fortune so vast that in gold alone, they owned an entire mountain."

"Lots of money in mountains of gold," said the generalissimo blandly. "Nice legend. I like legends."

"Suppose the legend is true. Suppose it is and suppose there is, hidden somewhere, that mountain of gold. It would make anyone the richest, most powerful person in the world. It's more important than oil because it is so spendable. No market prices being set at conferences. No delivery halfway across the world, like oil. Gold is pure wealth."

"Who's got this mountain?"

"We don't know who has it yet, but we know who rightfully owns it."

"Who?" asked Moombasa. He knew he was going to like this answer.

"You," said Lord Wissex. "It is Hamidian wealth."

"God's light shine through your eyes. Your mouth

speaks His truth," said Moombasa. Tears welled in his eyes. He looked to his generals and aides. They were all nodding. He would get them new uniforms. Medals with real gold in them. Maybe even the new electronic gear for torture. Every other country in South America had them. And himself? He would be able to live up to the name he had given himself: "the Great Benefactor." And he would be able to stash more gold in Switzerland than anyone else who had ever lived.

According to Lord Wissex, in America there was a woman who could read ancient Hamidian. An ancient plaque had been found and she had translated it to tell where the mountain of gold was. But she was keeping it to herself. And the evil Yankees were keeping her surrounded so she would lead them to the gold, the gold that was rightfully the natural property of the proud Hamidian people.

"The thieves," said Moombasa.

"Exactly," said Lord Wissex. "I'd like to interest you in the knife. The knife is basic. It is classic and, in this case, highly appropriate. Seven knife fighters of the highest quality and training, and guaranteed service by the House of Wissex, the greatest house of assassins in the history of the world. We deliver the girl and she delivers the gold and everything is neat and proper."

"Good. When I get the gold, you get the five million," said Moombasa.

"I'm sorry, General President, but we are not in the gold business. We are purveyors of violence and it is the tradition of the House of Wissex that we must be paid in advance, in cash."

"Five million dollars? You talking about ten tanks.

Or the education budget for the next five hundred years."

"How much do you want your gold?" Wissex asked.

"I give you two million."

"I'm awfully sorry, my friend, but you know we can't bargain. It's just not that sort of business."

"All right, but I got to get some blood too," said Generalissimo Moombasa Garcia y Benitez, President for Life and the Great Benefactor. "I ain't spending no five million dollars for no dry knife."

"All the blood you wish. You are, of course, the client," said Neville Lord Wissex.

Dr. Terri Pomfret was finally taking solid foods when the two walked into her hospital room and said they were her protection. At first she had thought they were patients.

The old Oriental could not have weighed a hundred pounds if his green kimono were sewn with lead. The white, obviously, was a manic hostile.

Rather handsome in a sinister way, of course, but hostile. Definitely.

He told her to stop eating the food because that would kill her faster than anything outside the hospital. Then he told her that he wasn't all that interested in her problems, her anxiety about height or depth, and as for anyone cutting anyone else's throat, she didn't have to worry, her throat was safe.

"I was assured I was going to get the finest protection in the country. Now who or what are you?" asked Terri Pomfret. She felt the tears coming up again behind her eyes. She wanted a tissue. She wanted another Valium. Maybe a dozen Valiums.

The old one said something in an Oriental language. She recognized it as Korean, but he spoke quickly and in an accent she had never heard so she could not translate.

What he had said and she didn't understand was: "What a disgrace! Once proud assassins and now nursemaids."

And the white answered in the same guttural accent. "Smitty says it's important. We've got to get a mountain of gold or something and this glutton can find it."

"We will be selling shirts on your street corners before that happens," said Chiun.

"What are you two talking about?" said Terri. She dabbed an eye with the tissue.

"We are discussing how lovely you are," said Chiun. "How your beauty radiates through your sorrowed eyes, how your travails bear down on not only a fine woman but a most beautiful one as well."

"Really?" asked Terri.

"What else would we say, gracious lady?" asked Chiun.

"Really?" said Terri to Remo. She was starting to like these two a bit.

"No," said Remo.

"What?" said Terri. "Did you say no?"

"Sure," said Remo.

"He cannot bear such loveliness," Chiun told her and then barked to Remo in Korean: "What is wrong the matter with you? You never understand women. First you go telling them things they don't want to hear and then you complain."

"I'm not at my best, you know. I've had such troubles——" Terri started.

Remo interrupted. "Why don't you tell us all about it on the way to the cave? We've got to check that inscription one more time before we go track it down, right?"

"Cave?" said Terri.

"The Albemarle Caves. Where everybody keeps getting cut into pieces," Remo said.

Terri smiled, excused herself, and then went blissfully into darkness.

She came to, unfortunately, in the wrong place. She was dressed and in the cave itself. She recognized the high ceiling and the dangling rope. She went immediately into shock and when she came to, she was in the arms of the man who was called Remo.

The Hamidian writing was coming down to her. Then she realized that she was moving up.

This Remo was climbing with one hand, as easily as if they were both walking up a flight of steps. He pulled, raised a hand, grabbed, then pulled again. Very quickly and very securely, even as he held her in one arm. She smelled the moisture at the top of the cave. She started to faint and then she felt his other hand do something to her spine.

She wasn't afraid.

She hadn't had a Valium and she wasn't afraid.

"What did you do?"

"Your fear was in your spine," Remo said.

"That can't be. It's emotional. My brain isn't in my spine."

"Don't bet on it," Remo said.

"It's working," said Terri. "I'm not afraid and I'm not taking Valium. But I'm here again." And suddenly, she did feel a pang of fear and the hand massaged her lower spine again.

"Stop doing it to yourself, okay?" said Remo.

"What? What?"

"Making yourself frightened. You're scaring yourself and pumping adrenalin into your body and that's stupid because you don't know how to use it anyway," he said.

"Okay," said Terri. "I'll try it. This feels great anyway. I've never been up here without fear before. I'll never be afraid again." She said it and she meant it and then she saw something and she screamed out her fear right in the stranger's face. People with knives were coming into the cave. Ugly curved knives. Agile people and she was on top of the cave, hanging from the wall, protected by two men who didn't even have weapons.

"Don't scream. He loves an audience," Remo said.

"The old man," yelled Terri in horror. "He'll be killed."

"It's Chiun," said Remo, "and if you keep quiet, he'll put them away quietly, but if he knows he's got an audience of someone he is serving, he'll waste time. He always does."

Terri saw the knife fighters surround the old man in the green kimono. She screamed: "Watch out behind you."

"That did it," said Remo with a sigh. "I suppose you want to watch."

She couldn't not watch. The kimono flowed, a Gurkha fell, the kimono danced like wind on the cave floor, first flowing, then circling and the knife fighters fell and tumbled like a carousel where all the horses on the outside suddenly collapsed at once. Finally there was only one and he lunged at the old man and the green kimono suddenly stuttered and then fell. He was dead.

"Eeeeeeeee," screamed Terri as Chiun fell.

The knife fighter plunged down, blade first, toward the green kimono, but then kept going into the silica sand of the cave bottom where he twitched and then stopped. The green kimono rose, and then did a bow to the upper reaches of the cave.

"See. I told you," said Remo. "We would have been down by now but you had to encourage a performance."

"I didn't even see his hands move," she said.

"You're not supposed to," said Remo. "If you had, we'd be dead."

On that word, Terri fainted again and came to with the inscriptions above her. She read them calmly. It was good that she had come back to the cave. She had missed one of the tell-tale punctuations and misread one word. Now she could place the mountain on the Yucatan peninsula, near the old Hamidian empire.

"You see the sign says that all gold from the country had to be moved to the Yucatan, because the mountain is the one safe place for the gold," Terri explained to Remo.

"Wrong," he said. "There is no safe place." He

repeated what he had learned a long time ago from Chiun. "The only safe place is in your own mind."

"How do I get there?" she asked.

"You got ten years and nothing else to do?" asked Remo and then he took her down the wall, again as easily as if descending stairs. On the soft sand floor, she said she didn't want to see any more bodies.

Four

Barry Schweid was giving *Hamlet* what Hank Bindle called "punch" when something strange came up on his word-processing computer.

Bindle had said he basically liked *Hamlet* but could Schweid improve Hamlet's character by having him win at the end?

"We don't want this 'to be or not to be' stuff. People don't like indecisive," Bindle had said.

"No box office in it. Never was," said Bruce Marmelstein.

"Instead of 'to be or not to be,' have him say what he is really thinking," Bindle had told Schweid.

"What's that?"

"I'm going to kill the guy who killed my father and is sleeping with my mother," said Bindle.

"The mother with the big jugs," said Marmelstein.

"Ophelia's got the jugs," said Schweid.

"No law against two women with a nice set each," said Marmelstein.

"Too much on the breasts. This is Shakespeare, you know. You have to respect it," Schweid insisted.

"Okay, Barry," said Bruce Marmelstein.

"But I'll give you him saying something about getting the man who is sleeping with his mother now," Schweid said.

"Right. We want the tension of *Jaws*, the excitement of *Raiders of the Lost Ark*," said Bindle.

"We're going to have a problem with people who know that Hamlet loses the big sword fight at the end. You know, there's somebody out here in Hollywood who's actually read the play and he says people won't like Hamlet losing."

"Lose?" said Bindle, shocked. "Nobody loses. The hero never loses."

"And he gets the woman with the tits," said Marmelstein.

"But Shakespeare's Hamlet loses," said Schweid. "I was told that."

"What lose? You want to make a hundred and fifty dollars doing an off-Broadway nothing?" said Bindle. "We're talking big bucks here. Big-budget picture. Nobody is going to do a big-budget picture about a loser."

"Legs. Ophelia's got to have legs," said Marmelstein. "But we've got an artistic problem. What about full frontal nudity?"

"Shakespeare was an artist," said Bindle. "We must stand up for his right to express his highest emotions, no matter what the cost to us personally."

"Sex act?" said Marmelstein. "Watch her and him balling on film?"

Bindle shook his head. "I said no matter what the cost. I didn't say getting an *x*-rating. That'll kill us at the box office. And you, Schweid, we want some winning violence. Make Hamlet the toughest mother ever to come out of England."

"Somebody told me he was Danish," said Schweid.

"I thought Shakespeare was English," said Bindle.

"Somewhere over there. Europe," said Marmelstein.

"Shakespeare was Danish," said Bindle. "Hmmmm."

"No. The character, Hamlet, was Danish," said Schweid.

"Big tits," said Marmelstein, who had been worrying about flat-chested English women. He had been thinking of using Swedes and dubbing in English voices. Now he could use Danish women with Danish-sized fronts.

"It's always acted by Brits," said Barry.

"Hey, we're doing your picture. Do us a favor. Get us what we need. We need the violence. We need Hamlet punching his way, fending his way through evil, protecting Ophelia, revenging his father's death," said Bindle.

So back to the word-processor computer went Barry Schweid and, in anger, he punched out calls for force, for violence, for destruction. And suddenly appeared on his screen the code system for reaching someone.

The code word was Shiva and Barry looked it up in the encyclopedia that had come with the house. Shiva was an eastern god, known as the Destroyer of Worlds.

He looked back at the computer. He saw patterns of training on a graph. He saw where an ancient house of assassins had created a single effective killing arm for a secret organization, the first white man ever to learn those skills. He knew that because there were some old questions more than a decade before about whether the student could learn. It was all right there on the TV screen.

What a fantastic idea, he thought. The greatest assassins that ever lived, tiny Orientals, infusing their knowledge and power into a white man. And why not? The white man could be Hamlet.

He was so excited he called Hank Bindle at home.

"Okay, we got it," yelled Barry into the telephone. "Hamlet gets training from assassins. The greatest assassin who ever lived. An Oriental."

"No," said Bindle.

"But the teacher is Korean, see. He's got to be Korean because this one house of assassins is the sun source of all the martial arts. You see, martial arts get weaker the more they get away from the original power these people taught. Everything else is an imitation. People saw these Koreans in action and imitated them. That's why all the martial arts come from the east."

"No way," said Bindle. "Chopsaki. Bruce Lee. A five million dollar picture that grosses fifteen million. We're talking about a twenty-two million budget. The guy has got to be white."

So Schweid made the teacher white. It didn't hurt, because he had the whole story. Right on the computer, there were hundreds of cases of intrigue and danger and how the pupil had created solutions through force.

Barry had the script done in three days. He thought it was grand, maybe even the best thing he had ever copied.

"No, absolutely not," said Bindle. "Where is the woman in danger? Where are Hamlet's problems?

You've got to think he can't make it before he makes it. Nobody is going to care about some guy who goes flip-a-finger and kills somebody. Have the finger break off. Have him bleed. Have him suffer. And then he wins."

"And gets the Danish broad with the big knobs," said Marmelstein.

"I like it," said Bindle.

"It'll jiggle," said Marmelstein.

But Barry Schweid was a bit nervous about returning to the computer. The story lines he had seen there had seemed real and in every one of them, people had really died. It explained many killings in the world which had been unsolved.

He looked at the computer reports for a long afternoon before deciding to plunge ahead. After all, how could it all be true? So many killings by one secret assassin?

And besides, he wasn't into politics. He was a creative artist, and he had a right to follow his muse, no matter what it told him to copy.

So he started writing.

Five

The gardener had been taking the unwanted rose blossoms for his daughter.

And so the gardener would die.

He would die piece by piece. The bullets would carve him like a chisel.

But save the legs for last. That would enable him to try to run.

The roses were just an excuse. Walid ibn Hassan needed to blood his new Mauser with the special .348 long barrel. There were those who preferred to use only paper targets before work, but those were lesser gunmen. They did not have tradition.

Back before guns, Walid's great-great-grandfather would not use a sword unless it had been cured in the body of a strong man, according to the Arab tradition for the manufacture of good steel blades. The Spaniards would use oil, and the Italians water to quench the red-hot steel of a sword.

But the really good steel, the Damascus blade of the Arabs, had to be quenched in blood.

Walid was enough of a realist to understand that the water in the blood did the quenching of the steel. But he also understood the real meaning of curing a blade like that. It meant the weapon was for killing. It was not for ornament and it was not for beauty. It was a killing tool.

And that was why, this day, in his mansion overlooking the blue Mediterranean of the Tunisian coastline, he waited for his gardener to steal one more rose.

The bushes were in blossom and the perfume blended with the vigorous salt of the Mediterranean and breezes coming in from Crete and Greece and the wondrous places where man first laid the foundations of Western thought.

Walid ibn Hassan saw the gardener's red and white checkered kaffiyeh come around the high stone wall. He saw it pause and go down as the man picked a rose blossom, go further and then down as he picked yet another.

Walid could have used the cook. The cook was stealing meat from the kitchen. But the cook was fat and could not run, so Walid waited for the gardener.

He saw the kaffiyeh go down, then up, then down, then up, and then the man came around the bend of the wall, smiling.

In his robe, he cradled seven perfect blossoms.

He came to Walid ibn Hassan and offered to show how beautiful they were.

"You grow the finest roses in Tunisia. Nay, the entire North African coast," the gardener said.

"Thank you, friend. You are not just a servant. You are a son to me."

"Thank you, Pasha ibn Hassan," said the gardener.

"But I only see seven blossoms."

"Yes," said the gardener. His eyes could not stay away from the gun.

"You bent down ten times."

"Did I, great Pasha?"

"Where are the other three blossoms?" Walid asked.

"They were not fit to grace your home. I have them in my pocket."

"And what do you do with those blossoms you keep in your pocket?"

"Those," the gardener said with a laugh, "those are not nearly good enough for your house. Not nearly. I give them to my daughter."

"You give *my* roses to your daughter. I have been like a compassionate father to you, and you take my roses in return?"

"But you would not use them, O Pasha."

"That is not for you to decide. When one takes a gift instead of waiting for it to be given, that then is stealing."

"Oh no, great one."

"Still I am compassionate and generous. I am your friend and a man of honor. You may run. I will not shoot you close-up for your thievery. Run."

The gardener fell to his knees, crying "Please."

"Run or I will shoot you here and you will see the end to my compassion."

The gardener stood up, trembling.

"Run," said Walid ibn Hassan and, true to his word, he did not fire until the man was fifty yards away. At that point, he sent a slug into the flailing left hand and got the first finger. At sixty yards he got the second finger and at seventy he had to take the hand. By a hundred yards, the hand was a stump on the wrist, breathing blood.

Hassan had the Mauser at his cheek and working well. She was a good gun. She took a piece out of the right shoulder, and at 180 yards when the distance was becoming too great for perfect accuracy, she put a perfect slug into the left knee.

It dropped the man. Hassan worked his beauty, quickly, before the man could die of blood loss. He took off the feet, changing clip after clip to keep shooting.

The gardener twitched and jerked each time Hassan's beauty sent a lead kiss across the grounds to their target. She tortured the man beautifully, even taking off his manhood, and when she was asked, she sent the gardener to eternity with a shot through the eye.

Walid ibn Hassan kissed his beauty on her grip and very tenderly put her into a velvet case. She was ready.

The gardener would be buried among the roses where his body could, in death, nourish the roots as he had in life.

Hassan had cured his weapon in blood.

He was ready. That afternoon he was on an airplane bound first to Mexico City and then to the nation of Hamidia. To get his beauty through all the airport checks, he had her disassembled into several sections; but finally, after the flight from Mexico by a small airplane to the People's Democratic Republic of Hamidia, he was at the gates of the People's Liberation Palace with his beauty, as he had been instructed to be.

Nine other men waited with their rifles.

"Hello, Mahatma," he said to the Indian. "Blessings upon you, Wu," he said to the Burmese.

"Walid, my brother," said the Ghanaian, dark as pitch with a killing eye that Walid knew was as accurate as a beam stretched to the dark side of the universe.

"What is it this time, Walid?" Wu asked.

"I do not know. Mahatma always knows."

Mahatma shrugged and readjusted his turban. "I do not know. But we always do well with Lord Wissex."

On this, everyone agreed.

They waited for half an hour in the hot Hamidian sun with the odors of Liberation City wafting to them from unfinished sewers. They did not mind this, mainly because their own countries were run remarkably like Hamidia. It was a requirement of the Third World that one's grandiose ambitions for a new world order were in inverse proportion to how well your government treated human waste. Thus sewers were delayed while delegates built the new infrastructures of world governments. This was best done, however, away from Third World countries because their streets stank. It was no accident that the Third World countries never moved the United Nations away from New York City.

Finally Lord Wissex emerged from the People's Palace.

"Are we all here?" he called out.

There were ten yeses amid wishes for his long health, the fecundity of his wife concerning male children, and various assorted gods wishing him all manner of eternal life and wealth.

"Thank you all," said Lord Wissex. "The House of Wissex has always relied on its loyal allies and friends in its hour of need. We are assured by your faithful service of your good wishes and we see fine fortune ahead for all in these endeavors upon which we now embark."

There was general applause.

"We have been called upon to defend the natural rights of the independent nation of Hamidia—which we will do," said Wissex. "And do forthrightly."

"Hear, hear," came voices from the ten gunmen.

"Tally ho," said Lord Wissex. "Follow me." All ten snipers marched into the courtyard and then into the palace, where Generalissimo Moombasa sat brooding with his general staff.

"Rifles," he said to Wissex in disgust. "I got thousands of rifles."

Walid ibn Hassan heard his precious loved one called a "rifle." He said nothing; nor did the others. He had been in situations like this before and Lord Wissex had explained:

"In situations like this, talk not with your tongue but with your weapon. And I will decide when that talks."

But Hassan did not need Lord Wissex to explain this. His father had told him this. And his grandfather had told his father and his grandfather had been told by his great-grandfather.

For the family of Hassan had worked for the House of Wissex for many generations. In days gone by, way in the past, Hassan knew, a man would pledge himself to a king's service and when the king prospered, the man would prosper. But when the king fell, so did the man. He would lose everything.

Then one day, an Englishman had arrived in Tunisia looking for the best rifle shot and when it was shown to be a Hassan, he explained to the man a new way of doing things. One did not serve a single king, but one provided a service to any king. One worked for gold. Gold never failed. Gold was never assassinated or defeated in battle or ever betrayed its owner one dark night with poison in a friendly-looking cup. All eyes smiled on gold and never was the revolution that had overturned it.

Gods disappeared before man's love of gold. Give Lord Wissex your rifle and Lord Wissex would give you gold. After, of course, proper commissions were taken by the House of Wissex. Lord Wissex had not come to the shores of Tunisia as a charity.

Through the years, the House of Wissex had been proved right, so Hassan waited, letting the insults pour from the semiliterate South American dictator. As did Mahatma and Wu and the Ghanaian and all the other snipers. They had heard insults before, but they always got paid.

"I use my own rifles. Why I gotta pay you, Wissex? Millions?"

"Because these are not just rifles," said Lord Wissex coolly. "These are prime-quality snipers."

"Already I got snipers. You hang in a tree and you shoot someone in the head."

"Would you like a demonstration?" asked Wissex.

"Sure. You. Carlito. General Carlito. Shoot that nigger in the face." He pointed to the Ghanaian.

General Carlito wore dark sunglasses and many shiny medals. Walid ibn Hassan could hear the medals shaking.

General Carlito spoke. "You there. Captain. Shoot the nigger."

And the captain spoke.

"You there. Sergeant. Shoot the nigger."

And the sergeant, looking at the Ghanaian's fine rifle, and remembering tales of what happened when Wissex's knife fighter had come to the palace, jumped out the first floor window and ran.

"Must I do everything myself?" said Generalissimo Moombasa. He put his right hand on his pistol and with his left hand pointed to Hassan, who was holding his beloved one in his fingers in front of him.

"You there," said Moombasa and Hassan stepped forward.

Moombasa stared at him with Latin dark eyes. A deadly smile crossed his face. His weight balanced evenly on both feet. His hand rested on the pistol as light as a bird, but as deadly as a hawk.

"You there," said Moombasa again and beckoned slowly with a left finger. Moombasa's officers stepped aside lest a bullet stray, a bullet heading for their beloved generalissimo.

"You there," said Moombasa, his voice now even arrogant. "Shoot that damned sergeant who jumped out the window."

The Hamidian general staff applauded.

"We got to keep discipline," said Moombasa. The general staff agreed. Without discipline, man was nothing. Discipline, said one colonel, separated man from beast.

"You got a point there," said the generalissimo.

Hassan walked casually to the window, raised his gun in a smooth motion, and fired as soon as it reached his cheek.

The Hamidian general staff thought he had made a mistake, that the gun had gone off accidentally. They had not even seen the Tunisian aim.

"You want another shot?" said Moombasa.

"Excuse me, Generalissimo," said Lord Wissex. "He hardly needs that, what?"

"What?" said Moombasa.

"Doesn't need that, what?"

"What? What what?" asked Moombasa.

"Please come to the window," said Lord Wissex.

The entire general staff moved to the window and there, lying at the wall of the palace courtyard, was the sergeant with a single shot in the back of his head.

"What you call that thing?" said Moombasa, pointing to the weapon in Hassan's hands.

"Beloved," said Hassan.

"Yeah. Where they sell them beloveds? Looks like a Mauser to me."

"Excuse me," said Lord Wissex. "The hiring of the tool includes the man."

"Can I shoot that thing?" Moombasa said.

"I am afraid that is one thing I cannot sell you," Wissex said.

"All right then. The rifleman," Moombasa yelled. "But I want that mountain of gold. I was assured that the knife fighters wouldn't fail."

"I beg your pardon," Wissex said, "but not so, sir. What we assured you was that we provided the finest knife fighters there are."

"This time I want success."

"You are getting the best," said Lord Wissex.

"Make sure," said Moombasa, and while Hassan and the other snipers marched out, Wissex finalized the contract. Five million dollars more.

Before the snipers set off, Wissex described the woman they were to seize. Apparently, there was some obstruction, he said, some bodyguards that were better than the usual thick-witted musclemen.

"You there, Mahatma, you will be in charge. I want to know what the bodyguards are like, before you destroy them. But seize the girl unharmed."

And then Wissex took out a map and showed where the woman and her bodyguards would be going. It was a small village in the Yucatan peninsula.

"They will be going to this village. Camping over probably. And then on to this area over here, where the woman may find an inscription. That might be the best point because they will all be concentrating on that inscription. Do you understand?"

"Spoken is done," said Mahatma.

There were other things Terri Pomfret didn't like besides heights and depths. She didn't like mosquitoes. Some said the Yucatan grew them with bellies like baseballs and beaks like railroad spikes.

"How come he isn't bothered? Or you?" she said to Remo. They had stopped four times for her to rest.

"Because, like the forces of the universe, mosquitoes respect the good," Chiun said. "However, they do not bite Remo because I have taught him tricks."

"Teach me tricks," said Terri.

"Why?" said Chiun.

"Because I'm not going any farther unless you do," she said.

"Then sit and stay here. We have promised to keep you alive, not comfortable," Chiun said.

"Why did you have to say that to him?" Remo asked Terri.

"What difference does one more insult make in a life?" Chiun interrupted. "They are like the mosquitoes. Killing one does no good, nor is it missed."

"What insult? What insult did I say?" screamed Terri. Her skin bitten, her legs raw from the sweating pants, the jungle so humid it was like swimming; and now to top it all, the Oriental was angry at her.

"Well, you wouldn't think it's an insult," Chiun said.

"Of course I don't think it's an insult. I don't even know what it is," she said.

"How crude. How white," said Chiun.

"I didn't say it," Remo said.

"No. This time you didn't. But your friend did."

Remo was mad. Terri Pomfret wasn't his friend. She was a very talky professor who had to be escorted to some make-believe mountain of gold. But early on, when he had had trouble convincing her that she would be safe, Chiun had decided that she was Remo's friend. That way, he could add her actions to Remo's and keep brimming the bowl of the world's injustices to a kind, decent old man wishing only peace. It sometimes could keep Remo in line.

But this time, Remo had decided it was not his fault and she was not his responsibility. And he was going to do the job because it was his job. No more. She was not his friend, and he wouldn't take that baggage from Chiun. Even if she was attractive when she wasn't yelling as she was now.

"Will you, for heaven's sakes, please, please, please tell me what insult I committed. Just tell me. I won't do it again."

"It's nothing," said Chiun.

"No. Tell me. Please tell me. So I will never do it again."

"If you wish and only because you beg. I should be addressed as 'Gracious Master.' "

"Certainly, Gracious Master. Absolutely, Gracious Master."

And Chiun raised a finger so that the long nail was perpendicular to his shoulder.

"Correct," he said. "See, Remo. I have just met this noisome woman and already she knows how to address me."

"I'm not calling you Gracious Master," Remo said.

"And after all I have given him," Chiun told Terri.

"Why don't you call him Gracious Master if that's all he wants?" Terri asked.

"You don't understand," Remo said. "Let's go."

"And now *you're* mad," Terri said to Remo.

"Sweetie, if you want to go through life with everyone liking you, better dig a hole and end it now because that isn't going to happen," he said.

Terri slapped her neck. There was another mosquito bite. Chiun picked three leaves and told Terri to chew them.

"The Chocatl chew them from birth and mosquitoes never bother them. A good people, the Chocatl. In your calendar of 907, we serviced the Chocatl, although they were somewhat poor. We took carvings instead of gold. The Incas had gold. The Mayans had gold. But not the Chocatl. But because they showed proper respect for a Master of Sinanju, we killed the evil king who was persecuting these good people. Even though they had no gold. Only carvings."

"That's a beautiful story. But I thought the Americas were only discovered in the 1400s," Terri said.

"By white men," Chiun explained.

"Why didn't you share your knowledge with the world?" Terri asked.

"Open up a market to competitors?" Chiun said.

"I think that is very beautiful about serving someone for only carvings because that was all they could afford. It makes even assassins look noble. Not that I have anything against what you do," Terri said.

"We are often misunderstood," said Chiun. He looked at Remo, but Remo was looking up ahead. This was supposed to be a village trail, yet there were no signs of anyone having walked the path in the last few hours—which they would certainly find if they were close to a village. There were no freshly snapped twigs or pressed foliage from feet that left ever-so-minute impressions on the cells of the leaves.

"Don't you think that is beautiful?" Terri asked Remo.

"About the carvings of the Chocatl?" Remo said.

"Yes."

"Have you seen them?" Remo asked.

"No. Of course not."

"Ask him what those carvings were made of," Remo said.

He tried to get the sense of the village up ahead as Chiun had taught him. One could feel a concentration of people if one let the body do it. You didn't force the listening or you would never hear. You let what was be, and in being, you understood it was there. But the path was widening and there was no village up ahead. How he knew, he could not explain. But like so much of Sinanju, it just was.

There was something up ahead but it wasn't a friendly village.

"What were the carvings made of?" Terri asked, chewing the leaves and happily surprised that mosquitoes now seemed to try to avoid her.

"A nothing," Chiun said. "Certainly not gold."

"He says nothing," she told Remo.

"Since when is jade nothing?" said Remo. He raised a hand for a halt.

"Jade? The carvings were jade? And you said they were nothing," Terri told Chiun.

"You can think of jade as nothing," Chiun said blandly.

"No one else does."

"When you are used to working for gold and settle for less, then jade is nothing. It is nothing compared to your lovely smile," Chiun said.

"Do you mean that?" Terri asked. Her head turned toward Chiun, she bumped into Remo.

"Hey. You interested in living? Stop," said Remo.

"How could I not mean it?" Chiun asked Terri.

"I've been told my smile is my best feature," Terri said. She felt a hand on her shoulder. Remo was pointing for her to step back.

"It always is with the really great beauties," Chiun said.

"I've never thought of myself as a great beauty. Attractive maybe. Stunning perhaps," said Terri Pomfret. "But not really a great beauty. Not really. Not all the time, anyway."

"When the Master of Sinanju says great, he means great," said Chiun. "I have seen stunning and attractive. You are far beyond that."

"Hey, Terri. Death. Destruction. Fear. Getting killed. Valium. Heads rolling. Fingers cut off. Danger," said Remo, trying to get her attention.

"Yes," said Terri, giving a very special smile to Chiun. "Did you want something, Remo?"

"I want to save your body."

"Oh, yes. That. Thank you. Your teacher is such a wonderful person. I am so glad I got to know how really decent a true assassin is."

"Step back. That's it. Thank you," said Remo.

"I mean, most people think assassins are just killers, you know. They don't take time to really know them."

"Back," said Remo.

"They judge without knowing. And that is just ignorance," she said.

"Beautiful woman, he is working. Please step back with me," said Chiun.

"I didn't notice," she said apologetically.

"Yes," said Chiun. "Three direct threats can be very subtle."

Remo moved on up the trail. He wanted to be alone for this. He wanted to move alone. He was quiet with the trail but the birds were not calling. He was quiet with the trail but the noises of people where there should be noises were not coming up the trail.

He had not done much training in the countryside because, as Chiun had explained, major work was almost always done in cities because that was where the rulers were.

Yet the way to knowing the jungle was knowing oneself. One knew the sea by one's blood. One knew the jungle by one's breath.

Remo moved like a midnight dream, silent with all that was around him because he *was* part of all that was around him. Long ago, before he had been recruited for this training, in a time of beer and bowling alleys and hamburgers with cheese on them and sugar and tomato sauce, he would have thought of a place like the jungles of the Yucatan as bushes that should be removed.

Now, as a part of it, he was sure of it.

"I hate this junk," he mumbled to himself, looking at the broad green leaves and bright flowers. "Pot this place, plant some grass and make it a golf course or a park."

A bowling alley, he thought, would look nice around here. Anything would look nice here except this jungle. That was what he thought when he saw the outlines of a man in camouflage combat fatigues. Man had a gun. Another sniper on the small ridge surrounding the trail that entered the village. Lookouts.

Remo moved off the trail and skirted the two snipers. He would have liked to have moved up a tree for a look into the village but high things for men who were preparing a trap always attracted notice. Underbrush was safe.

He moved low through that until he came to the clearing. The clearing reminded him that people did not really ever live in the jungle because they always had to clear space for their villages.

And then he saw the pit. He knew what was in there because no one was moving in the village. All the villagers had been killed and put in that pit. And then leaves had covered it.

It had to be recent, within the last few hours, because human bodies rotted quickly. It was one of the few species that almost always had food in its stomach.

There were more men. A few surrounded the village but the greater concentration were at the small hillock to the south, the one with a black craggy rock sticking out of it, as if someone had brought it in from Colorado and stuffed it into the jungle.

Remo counted ten men in all.

The main body was at the large black rock. They also had a spring net as if they were going to capture some animal. The important thing, Remo told himself, was not to let any one of the snipers go wandering off. One of them might just throw a shot down the trail, which would be no problem for Chiun but might hurt Terri.

Ten, thought Remo and moved up behind the

first very quietly. The sniper was lying in prone position, the rifle resting on his palms. Remo severed the spinal column just beneath the cranium. The sniper went to sleep on his rifle forever.

Remo caught the next sitting lotus-like with the gun in his lap. Remo moved his left hand to the throat and with the concentrated power some might ascribe to a steam shovel kept the man seated with more and more pressure until the back cracked.

He put away two more who were scanning the long trail with binoculars. He simply put the binoculars into the heads with a smothered slap into the lenses. The eye sockets kept going.

Remo heard a little tune in his head. It was "Whistle While You Work" and he hummed it softly.

Walid ibn Hassan waited with his beloved, trained perfectly on the trail before him. He had not heard on his small radio from Mahatma for twenty minutes. That was strange. Mahatma had been the first point on the trail and had seen them. Three of them, an Oriental, a woman, and a white man.

He had beamed that in on the shortwave to Lord Wissex's man at a station nearby, and Hassan had picked it up on his radio. This was necessary because Wissex wanted to know what the bodyguards were like. Hassan knew why. He had heard that knife fighters had been killed by these bodyguards and now here he was. It was the old rule: first knives, then guns.

So Hassan kept his beloved ready, barrel pointed down the trail, eyes alert. He remembered what he had heard of the dead knife fighters and alone among the snipers he did not regard this as just another easy mission.

And alone among all the snipers Walid ibn Hassan saw 2:30 P.M.

And then a man was standing right in front of him, as if dropped by magic in the middle of the trail, so close that Hassan could not use the scope. He was a thin man with thick wrists and dark eyes and he was smiling.

"Hi. Nice jungle, isn't it?" said the man. He was American so he must be one of the three. But Hassan did not wait to make sure.

In every other service he had performed for Wissex, he had been careful to be exactly right about the target. But this time, he knew no one would punish him for shooting first. So he let his beloved kiss the man's chest. That would fell him. Then he would let his beloved kiss the white man's eyes and then his mouth. Those were Hassan's plans for the next shots.

But the first shot did nothing. The trigger was pulled and the man seemed to move even before the thought of the shot. He was standing sideways. Hassan squeezed off two more shots where the man's eyes had been, realizing that the man moved again even as his beloved was firing.

Hassan was now shooting without even aiming, pulling the trigger madly, until his beloved left his hands.

The man was standing over him, pawing his beloved.

"What do you call this thing?" Remo asked, noticing how well-polished the rifle was.

"Beloved," cried Walid ibn Hassan, reaching for

the precious one that would return his honor in blood.

"I could never tell these things apart. I don't even know the names of guns, you know," said Remo. "A man who uses a gun, well, that means he doesn't have it within himself. But, honest, it's a pretty gun. Okay, sweetheart. Party's over," said Remo and Hassan felt his beloved's barrel puncture his belly with eye-popping pain.

Hassan dared not move because any movement increased the pain. He felt the barrel go higher, into his chest cavity, even to his breathing, and then he noticed he was high off the ground. The man was carrying him easily, high above the ground as a waiter would carry a tray and just as easily.

He was bringing Hassan back to the village where they had killed everyone—impaled on his beloved.

He was bringing him to that Oriental sign that the Chocatl chief had been pointing to as some form of protection. The chief had been the first to die with Hassan sending a kiss from his beloved to the man's forehead. The chief was now at the bottom of the pile in the pit. He had died still pointing to that symbol carved in jade before his hut.

Hassan was now being lowered to that sign, his face very close to it.

"See that? In Korean, that means house or House of Sinanju. Just house will do. It's become sort of a trade name in the past few thousand years. It means that this village was protected by the House of Sinanju, except we blew it, and protection is impossible since you've already killed everyone.

However, the House of Sinanju is also big on meaningless vengeance. Do I have the safety on?"

"What?" grunted Hassan.

"Hold it. No, I don't think so. I think the safety will move. Yes."

And Walid ibn Hassan's beloved sent a kiss up through her master's brain, taking off a piece of cranium.

Remo discarded the gun and impaled owner in the bushes and returned to Chiun and Terri.

"I made a perfect shot with a rifle," Remo said to Chiun. "Got the brain easily. Dead center."

"You shot a man?" said Terri, aghast.

"Only one. There were nine others I didn't shoot," Remo said.

"Well, that's encouraging," Terri said.

"I don't like guns," Chiun said.

"Of course not," said Terri, gushing over the man in the kimono. "You're too gentle of heart, Master of Sinanju."

"Guns breed bad habits," Chiun said.

"I knew you were really against violence," Terri said. "Why is it people don't realize assassins abhor violence? It's the press. Ignorant and shallow as ever."

"An occasional shot won't hurt," Remo said.

"One is too much," Chiun said. "Even one. The first can lead to a second and then you will be using it for your livelihood and losing everything I taught you."

"Beast," said Terri, looking at Remo.

Barry Schweid had the greatest adventure script he had ever seen, right from the computer tales of the greatest killing weapon in the form of a human being.

"Stunning," was the one word he thought appropriate.

"Won't work," said Hank Bindle. "We need feminine jeopardy. We need him struggling and suffering. So you don't know who is going to win."

"You thought Superman was going to lose?" asked Schweid.

"*Raiders of the Lost Ark*," intoned Bindel.

"*Starwars*," added Marmelstein. "And think of what they could have made if they'd had a few nice boobs in there."

"But how do you make superweapons ordinary?" asked Schweid.

"Not ordinary," said Bindle. "Vulnerable."

"With shirts getting ripped," said Marmelstein.

"Hey, what about the hero walking down the street alone when all his friends desert him?" Schweid suggested. "And he is the only one left to face the killers."

"That's too weird," said Bindle. "Can't sell it."

"*High Noon*," said Schweid.

"There you go again. When we say we want original and we want fresh, we don't want you to copy the oldies. That's too far out. Copy what everybody else is doing now," said Marmelstein. He fingered the chains around his neck, then shouted, "That's it! Something really really new. I've got it."

"What have you got?" asked Bindle, and then said to Schweid, "When Bruce Marmelstein has an idea, it's always a great one."

"For years now we have been waiting until a

film is a success before we capitalize on what the box office tells us," Marmelstein said. "Why wait?"

"What are you talking about?" asked Bindle, suddenly worried.

"Why not steal the major scripts before they are made and then we come out a week before with our own productions?"

"Thank God," said Bindle, weakly seeking a chair in the office. He had to take the weight off his legs for a moment. He had thought his partner was going completely berserk. The pressure in Hollywood could do that.

"Thank God," Bindle said again, now breathing easily. "For a minute, I thought you were actually going to suggest we make up something new."

"You mean, really new? Out of thin air?" said Marmelstein. "Why would we want to do that? We're producers, not some cockamamie writers in the East. Bindle and Marmelstein stand with Hollywood tradition. We will never produce what is not tried and true. We will never do anything that hasn't been done before. You want inventions, go to General Electric. We're movie makers."

"Movie makers," said Bindle. It made him feel in some way noble, part of a great tradition stretching back through generations of copiers and idea-thieves.

"Getting back to the point," said Schweid, "you want the trainer to be white, right? And you want his pupil to be not so good, sort of vulnerable. And you want big breasts."

"Just write in women. I'll take care of the breasts," said Marmelstein.

"Women in jeopardy," said Bindle.

"With ripped shirts," said Marmelstein.

"What about a big-breasted Hungarian woman trained to be the killing weapon for a secret U.S. government agency?" suggested Schweid.

"What are you talking about? Nobody's ever done that," said Marmelstein.

"I'm giving you what you want."

"I want box office. I want the gross over four hundred million," said Marmelstein.

"But those things come *after* you make the movie, not before," said Barry Schweid.

"Oh," said Marmelstein.

Six

Neville Lord Wissex waited for the message that would tell him the woman had been captured.

Already his plans had been formulated. He would turn her over to Moombasa, and then—at a fair market price—provide her with escorts so she could travel around the world looking for the mountain of gold.

As he totaled up the costs on a yellow pad on his desk, he felt pleased with himself. He had expected a rock-bottom minimum of five million dollars. When his knife fighters had been bested, the price had risen to ten million. Even for the House of Wissex, it was a very tidy sum, and it would enable them to carry on while he was promulgating similar large schemes. And it saved the house all the trouble of racing around to unmanageable countries with unpronounceable names to silence dissidents, all in the name of anti-imperialism.

It was the new direction that the young Lord Wissex envisioned for the ancient house: big projects with big returns.

He waited all afternoon and no radio operator picked up any signal.

The agent who had been waiting within radio range of the group in the Yucatan phoned at what was midnight for him and predawn in London with a report that there was complete radio silence out of the Yucatan. Not even a peep. He was heading in toward the village.

Wissex examined the description of the bodyguards again. He had fed it into his computer terminal in the London townhouse and now he tried to pull from the machine the probable source and probable training of the bodyguards.

The House of Wissex knew how the KGB, how the American FBI, CIA, and Secret Service trained. How MI5 trained. He could spot someone trained by any of them, and he could spot even the freelance terrorists because all had their little idiosyncracies. Some did well against knife fighters. Others did well against snipers. But according to the information coming back from the computer, only one agency did well against both.

That was the Swiss secret agency, perhaps the best in the world, and certainly the most secret. They guarded Swiss banking interests all over the world and on those rare occasions that a cover was blown, they managed to sew another back on immediately, no matter who or how many were killed. The real beauty of the Swiss was that they did things so quietly; none of their killings ever made the press.

Competent and discreet. These two bodyguards for the American woman could have been working for the Swiss, but they only employed Swiss nationals. And one of the two bodyguards was described as a frail old Oriental in a kimono. Not even close to a hundred pounds. And the other was an American. No particular pattern to their walking, except there seemed to be a smooth shuffle. And a lot of talking.

Wissex waited for the report from his agent in the Yucatan. A message had come in from Generalissimo Moombasa reporting that "all freedom-loving liberated peoples cheer the heroic struggle for the return of the inalienable rights to their ancient, just resources of the Hamidian people. Vanguard Revolutionary Suicide Battalion awaits your command."

Basically, this meant that Moombasa wanted to know how the capture had gone so he could get on with his search for the gold. It also meant that someone named Myra Waxelburg had left her home in Scarsdale, New York, because of an argument with her parents over who would get the Mercedes Benz one evening, and Myra had taken it upon herself to volunteer her services to the Hamidian embassy in their honorable revolutionary struggle against the oppressive forces of capitalism. Like her parents who had just told her that she had to use the Porsche because they needed the Mercedes Benz that night.

It was Myra's conviction that anyone the *National Review* called a tinhorn dictator had to be a revolutionary hero.

So Myra and her friend, Dudley Rawlingate III, heir to a chemical fortune, had volunteered their services to Moombasa and ever since, he was trying to palm them off on the House of Wissex, as the

Vanguard Revolutionary Suicide Battalion, in an attempt to reduce his bill.

Wissex cabled back.

"Congratulations on readiness of your Vanguard Revolutionary Suicide Battalion. They also serve who only stand and wait . . . elsewhere."

Then back to deadly business in the Yucatan.

Finally, Wissex's agent reported.

"All operatives dead, one grotesquely with brain blown out from below. No apparent harm to woman and her two bodyguards. Bodies of our men being examined. Initial pathologist report indicates something with the force of a hydraulic machine crushed bones and penetrated brains, but no marks of weapons or machinery found."

Lord Wissex returned to Wissex Castle to think. He did not like London for thinking. One used London for gaming. For business. But not for thinking. One did not think well in a noisy crowded place.

To really think, Wissex needed the battlements of home and the winds blowing over the countryside that his family had ruled for so long.

The problem was obvious. Someone had invented a new machine.

It was portable and it did not use a projectile. But then how could it destroy ten snipers? Perhaps a form of force field.

Had anyone been working on something like that? Should he look for that? Should he back away? Had any of his now dead men given him away? Would these two strange bodyguards with the deadly new machine come after him?

Would he have to face them himself? If so, with

what? But even as he asked the question, he knew the answer. He had counted on Moombasa's stupidity to finance one five-million-dollar score for the House of Wissex, and already the greedy dictator had paid for two. If two, why not more? And Wissex would keep squeezing the insolent turnip until he had drained every cent he could out of the dictator, and, in the process, had killed the two bodyguards. If indeed they were even alive at the moment.

So engrossed was the young Lord Wissex in his thoughts that he did not hear his uncle Pimsy hobble up the stone steps with his trusted poodle Nancy. He did things with that dog that the Wissexes did not talk about. No one interrupted Uncle Pimsy, however, because if he didn't have the poodle, he might have to go back to little boys and girls. And that always caused a ruckus of sorts.

Lord Pimsy was nationally known as the founder of Children Scouts, a Britannic approach to nature and youth. It had 3,000 members before anyone found out what Uncle Pimsy was doing at those camps that he provided for London's "city-bound waifs."

Quite a scandal but as British scandals went, it was good for only a week until some other lord was found with all those bodies he had promised to bury free. Hadn't buried them at all, but kept them in a freezer locker in his basement. Two hundred of Her Majesty's subjects had to be thawed, washed, reclothed, and buried. Bit of a mess.

"Problem, Neville?" harrumphed the old Lord Pimsy.

"Business," said Neville.

"Steel. Good British steel. Honest steel. Steel."

"Thank you, Uncle," said Lord Neville.

"British steel. You can count on it."

"Yes, Uncle."

"Steel to the gut."

"Well, Uncle, it's a bit more complicated than that," said Lord Neville.

"Nothing is so complicated that good British steel can't cut through," said Uncle Pimsy.

"We've already used knife fighters and failed."

"Knife fighters?"

"Our trusty Nepalese Gurkhas."

"Wogs. Can't use wogs. Good British steel with English lads behind them. Will take the measure of any man."

"Yes, that is an option."

"Option? It's your course, boy. Charge."

"Yes, well, thank you, Uncle. How's Nancy?'

"Bit off her feed but a fetching lass, isn't she?"

Pimsy petted the poodle who wearily stood her ground as she was trained to do.

"Uncle Pimsy, we are up against a new machine that we can't fathom. It is a new age. There are no more kings to service, no more crowns in the West to assure. This is a new world. With new machines and new clients."

"Your wogs again, boy," said Uncle Pimsy.

"The wogs have the need and the money, Uncle. The industrialized world has its own in-house staff. They don't need us. If we went to Number 10 Downing Street and offered our services, they would laugh us out. Yes, wogs."

"Steel's good against wogs. But powder's better. The little yippie beasts run at the big bangs."

"Not anymore, Uncle. We can't survive murdering girl-friends for Henry VIII forever."

"That's a lie," said Pimsy heatedly. "We put away one embarrassment and our enemies have bruited it about for the past three centuries. And you believe them. You've always thought the worst of the Wissex. I don't mind telling you, I was against your taking over. Yes. There you have it. Out in the open. The truth."

'You've been telling me that every month for the past seven years, Uncle."

"Have I? Well, doesn't hurt to restate it."

"Yes, but we have grown rather wealthy in that time. And look. My hands are clean," said Neville. "I have never skulked in an alley or had people blazing at my backside as I ran from an open window."

"You demean the name of Wissex."

"You're not limping, Uncle, because someone didn't get a round off at you."

"Honorable wound," Uncle Pimsy sputtered. "On an honorable mission. Not like these things you have the house involved in now. Fleecing some towel-head with the brains of a porcupine. Frightful form, Neville. Mine was an honorable wound."

"And you got an honorable seven thousand pounds for it, and already this week, I've made ten million dollars for our House from that towel-head Moombasa as you call him. And now I have a problem with a machine that fires no projectile, yet crushes bones, is so portable that no traces of it exist, and can be worked by one of those wogs you complain about and a white. That is what I have to wrestle with while you play with your doggy and talk of the old days."

"A wog?"

"Yes, wog," said Lord Wissex.

"What kind of wog?"

"Oriental."

"What kind of Oriental?" asked Uncle Pimsy.

"I don't know."

"What was he wearing?"

"Clothes, I imagine," said Wissex.

"What kind of clothes?"

"I think a kimono of some sort."

"Neville, lad, find the design of that kimono," said Uncle Pimsy. His voice was suddenly low. The bluster was gone and the old man was deadly serious.

"What does the pattern have to do with anything?" asked Lord Wissex.

"If it is what I am thinking of, those killings were not done by any machine. And your wogs may or may not have even seen what killed them."

"What are you talking about?"

"Find out the pattern of that kimono because we might all be dead if you don't know it," said Uncle Pimsy.

"You're serious, aren't you? You know, this isn't the Britannia-rules-the-waves sort of heroics."

"If that pattern is what I think it is, heroics or anything else won't do any of us any good."

"Would you mind telling me what you suspect?" Neville asked.

"Do you remember that your late father and I had one stipulation before you took over?"

"Yes. That we not take any contracts in the Orient. No clients in the East," said Wissex.

"Do you know why?"

"Frankly," Lord Wissex said, "I thought it rather peculiar but I had to make that promise so you wouldn't stop me."

"We had you make that promise because our fathers had us make that promise because their fathers had them make that promise because their fathers had them make that very same promise."

"What are you talking about?"

"I am talking, lad, about why you must find out the pattern of that kimono."

"You won't tell me beforehand?"

"Find it," ordered the old man, and he turned and limped his way down the battlements, with the poodle following behind wagging her scented tail.

"What a lovely kimono," said the British gentleman to the trio on the beach in front of the St. Maarten village of Grand Case. Grand Case was a walk up the road to the new headquarters front, the offices of Analogue Networking Inc. Smith had devised a plan whereby a request for the lost information would be beamed over the satellite during a weather disturbance similar to the one in which it had originally been lost. The hope was that it would reach the same terminus it had reached before. If it reached anyone. If all the records even existed anymore.

The request for return of the records had been carefully written by Smith, so as not to sound desperate. Instead, it hinted at a sizable reward. Nothing so big as to alarm, but enough to get interest from someone out there who might just be wondering what was all this nonsense about two decades of undercover work and its detailed portraits of how crime worked, with its names and numbers and tools and secrets to see a nation through its desperate years of trial.

So Remo and Chiun had returned to St. Maarten with Terri from the Yucatan, along with a battered golden plaque that they had found in an underground cave near the wiped-out village. Terri had to translate the plaque and its battered condition made that a detective's riddle, and so Remo, while waiting, would keep an eye on the transmission from Analogue Networking Inc. If something happened with CURE's records, Chiun would continue with Terri, and Remo would be off to retrieve the program.

Terri wore a scanty bathing suit while she pored over the rubbing of the Hamidian plaque they had found. Each time she thought she had the key to it, she had another question and it all still puzzled her.

She looked up from the rubbing as the cultured voice intruded on her thoughts.

"I say, that is an interesting pattern on the kimono you are wearing, sir."

Remo looked at the man. He was carrying a small concealed weapon under his left armpit.

Chiun stared at the horizon, that clean line separating the Caribbean blue from the pastel sky.

"I say, that is a most interesting design. May I photograph it?"

"Why do you ask?" said Remo. "You could just

stand up the beach over there and photograph us. Why do you ask?"

"I just thought you might mind."

"We do. Thank you. Don't photograph," said Remo.

"Oh," said the gentleman. He wore a dark suit with vest and regimental tie. He carried an umbrella.

"I say, what is that?" he said, looking at the rubbing Terri was analyzing.

"It is an ancient Hamidian inscription," she said.

"Yes, yes. I seem to have seen that somewhere. Some time," he said.

"Where?"

"The Yucatan Peninsula, I believe it was. I don't imagine you've been there."

"Why, yes, I have," said Terri. He was so polite.

"Why, yes, I have," said Remo, imitating in sing-song Terri's voice. "Surprise."

Terri shot him a dirty look.

"What does it say?" the British gentleman asked Terri.

"Nothing much," said Terri.

"I see. The villagers there also worshiped a jade standard with a similar design to the one your gentleman friend is wearing."

"His name is Chiun."

"Hello, Chiun. How do you do."

Remo smiled. He knew why Chiun was staring implacably at the horizon. He did not wish even to honor this man by a look.

A delicate finger with the nail curving gracefully upward emerged from the kimono. Slowly, it signaled the gentleman to come closer.

Down went the forehead, up went the finger, with such speed that only Remo saw it.

So fast and clean was the stroke that at first no blood emerged, just a thin line where the forehead had been cut. Not deep but deep enough.

By the time the British gentleman knew what had happened, the blood had formed in tiny specks on his forehead, reproducing the symbol on Chiun's robe. It was the symbol that meant "house," and that meant the House of Sinanju.

It was not necessary to say more.

"Better wash your forehead with the salt water," Remo said.

"I beg your pardon?"

"You've been cut on the forehead."

"It just tickled."

"Not supposed to hurt," Remo said.

A gloved hand went up to the forehead and came back down with blood on it.

"What? Blood. Gracious. My blood."

"Wash it off. It's not deep," Remo said.

"Why did he do that?"

"You wanted the symbol to take back to your master, so now you've got it. It means greetings from the House of Sinanju."

"I can't believe Chiun would do that," said Terri, who had not seen the blow because the hand had moved too quickly.

"He did it," said Remo.

"You did it. And you are blaming it on him. Right? Right, Chiun? You wouldn't do something like that, would you?"

Chiun did not answer.

"I'm sorry," Terri said. "I interrupted your meditation, but your partner has been slandering you again."

The Briton stumbled to the water's edge and splashed salt water on his forehead, groaning.

"It's only the salt that stings," Remo said.

"Poor man," said Terri.

Remo got up and went slowly toward the gentleman and reached into where he was favoring his body, just under an armpit. He brought out a very nasty little Cobra pistol.

He showed it to Terri.

"See? He is not just an innocent beach stroller."

"You palmed the gun to justify your vicious attack," she said.

Remo tossed the gun back to the man who put it in his neat little nylon shoulder holster.

"I also planted the shoulder holster. Under his jacket," Remo said.

"Well, he wasn't firing it," said Terri.

"I've got to leave, Little Father," said Remo. "I'll be back soon."

"Don't hurry," Terri said.

Remo kicked sand in her face.

"Go lift weights," he said.

"Did you see what he did?" Terri said to Chiun, but the old Korean was not answering. He was looking at the skyline for a reason Terri or the British gentleman could never fathom.

Remo knew why.

Chiun was looking at the skyline because he liked the way it looked.

At Analogue Networking Inc., the technician explained to Remo the foolproof method of checking whether a transmission was received or sent and how the computer stored such information.

Remo did not understand the language the man used. There was a satisfied sort of chuckle in the man's voice as he went on about all the wonders of computers.

He explained that it was the weather's fault that the program was lost in transmission. Not the computer's. The computer did not make mistakes. It couldn't. No one had yet taught it how.

On that the man showed his molars.

Remo stood behind him as Smith's message came in from Folcroft in Rye, New York. It was beamed along the same situation in satellite figuration, the man explained to Remo.

There was even the storm.

Nothing appeared on the screen.

"Perfect," the man said. "We think it got to the other source. If it appeared here, it would not have worked. So it worked. Possibly."

The man punched in a "confirmed." Confirmation of the confirmation returned.

"Perfect," said the man again. He wore a white shirt and faded unpressed slacks and, of course, that satisfied smile.

"What is perfect?" Remo asked.

"How this worked."

"What worked?"

"The transmission through the satellite being disturbed in hopefully the same manner," the technician said.

"So it reached the same person it reached the last time."

"It reached someone. It may not be that person,

you see. The person can be wrong. The computer is not wrong. It chose the wavelength and everything else identical to what it was before."

"In other words," Remo said, "it is right but what happened possibly wasn't right."

"You're familiar with computers, then?" said the man, showing his molars again.

"No. What I'm familiar with is stupid. When I hear stupid, that I know. I recognize stupid."

"You're not calling the computer stupid?" said the man, worried.

"Why would I do that? It's perfect," Remo said. "It just doesn't do things that work out right for people, that's all. But it's always right, even if everything turns out wrong. Right?"

"Absolutely," said the man. He showed his molars again.

Neville received his agent at Wissex Castle. The man was distraught. Good regiment. Good school. Good blood, English of course, but distraught nevertheless.

"Sir, if I did not have my paramount mission of returning with the symbol you requested, I would have thrashed those blighters."

"They wounded you?" said Lord Wissex, staring at the large bandage on his agent's forehead.

"They humiliated me and I suffered it because I knew the House of Wissex comes before all. Before life, before honor, before love."

"You'll get your raise, Toady old boy," said Wissex.

"Thank you, sir," said the agent. Uncle Pimsy stood somberly by Neville's side.

"Do you have the symbol?" he asked. He was drooling slightly down his gray vest but Uncle Pimsy had been drooling for the past twenty years.

The agent reached up to his forehead and with a yank took the bandage off. His face showed its embarrassment.

"Thank God," said Uncle Pimsy.

"You mean it's not who you think it is?" asked Lord Neville.

"It is who I knew it was. But they are giving us another chance," Pimsy said. "That is a warning. That's how they send it to other assassins."

"We're not assassins, strictly assassins," said Neville.

"They are," said Uncle Pimsy, and after the agent was dismissed, the uncle explained why no Wissex had taken work in the Orient since the fifteenth century.

It had occurred to one Wissex that the Orient was rich, and a Thai king had offered an ox's weight in gold for anyone who would kill a neighboring Burmese chieftain who had been raiding the king's borders.

The chieftain used the hills so well no army could capture him, so the king decided on an assassin.

The Wissex knew he was as good as any man with broadsword, long bow, or even the new experimental powder-firing muskets.

So off he went into the jungles of Asia, Pimsy related. Tracked the tribe which, of course, would not hide from one man. Made it into the camp, got the chieftain's head and set off for Thailand with the Burmese tribe hot on his trail.

Strange thing happened, don't you know. Heads kept falling about him. Out of trees. From behind rocks. Everywhere. And when he investigated the bodies, he found they were all carrying weapons and they all wore the clothes of that Burmese tribe.

So the Wissex realized he was being protected by someone who could move faster than he could and could see people he couldn't.

When he reached the gates of the Thai king's palace, he was accosted by a Korean in a kimono.

"Along your trail, you have been given many heads that saved your life. Now I want that one. For with that one, I am paid." And he pointed to the head of the Burmese chieftain that the Wissex carried in a leather bag.

"But I took the head," said the Wissex. "I should get something for it. I am grateful for my life but I earn my living by this."

"My name is Wang and I am of the House of Sinanju and I let you work your England because your king is cheap. Take the pittances from Europe. But Asia is mine."

"I'm afraid I can't do that," said Wissex, drawing the great broadsword with which he had cleaved many a spine and smitten many a skull to quivering jelly.

He pulled a level stroke through the kimono's middle but it was as if he had struck air, for the kimono swished around the blade. He swung for the skull with a perpendicular smash, and the great broadsword that he had swung with such awesome fury in his years cracked harmlessly into the ground.

Wang was laughing.

Wissex drew the long bow. He could put an arrow through an eye at fifty yards. And this close, he could send it through the back of the skull. It hissed from his bow. And Wang's face was still there, laughing.

Wissex aimed for the chest. The chest did not move. The arrow went through. Or seemed to. But there was no blood, no rent in the kimono, just the rustling of the material settling down.

Each time he fired an arrow, the kimono seemed to settle down from a flurry he could not see or understand.

And each time the Korean called Wang moved closer until he was finally only a breath away.

Wissex drew his dirk and went for the chest, but all he felt was his arm enwrapped with the light flossy kimono.

And with every stab, Wang seemed to kiss his forehead with a prickly thing.

The Wissex realized Wang was making a mark on his forehead with his teeth. He felt hot blood cloud his vision and then he was flailing wildly into air. But such were the powers of this Korean that even when Wissex had seen, he could not touch.

He dropped his knife and waited to die.

But he did not die.

"Go ahead and kill me, you pointy-eyed son of a plagued she-cow," said Wissex.

And Wang laughed again.

"If I kill you, others of your family will return—for that is the business of your family, to seek gold for strength of singular arms. And then I will have to kill them, for all they will know is that none return and it will take generations before the message gets through. Now you can know and tell. I have placed the mark of my kimono on your forehead. Stand back. It is not for you."

"But I cannot see your kimono. I am blinded by blood."

"When the wound heals on your forehead, you will see the mark in your mirror. It is the same as on my kimono. And do not use that smelly wound poultice you carry. It almost made me retch as I circled you all the way from Burma."

"It's a good poultice. A third of the wounds heal perfectl——"

"It is an awful poultice," said Wang. "Two out of three die from it." And from mosses, he pressed a new poultice upon the wound and within three days it had healed miraculously leaving only the faint red outline of the House of Sinanju.

And that was the last Wissex to bear arms in Asia.

Thus spoke Uncle Pimsy, taking his nephew Neville to a secluded room in Wissex Castle. There, in an old dusty painting, was the Wissex who had ventured into the realm of the Thais.

And on his head was a faint mark.

It was the same mark borne by the agent back from the Yucatan, the agent who had suffered his cut in moves he did not see, as a warning.

"Sinanju lives," said Uncle Pimsy, desperately clutching Neville's arms. "Run, lad. Save the House of Wissex. They've spared us again."

But Neville was thinking. What Uncle Pimsy had told him was apparently that the Sinanju people, whoever they really were, were still confined to hand-fighting. No weapons. And they might not have faced any sort of modern technology. Really modern.

"What are you thinking, lad?" asked Pimsy.

"Nothing."

"For God's sake, Neville, do not challenge the awesome magnificence of the House of Sinanju. Withdraw from this foolish scheme to fleece this Moombasa creature. Return to the old days. To British steel. To honest labor."

Uncle Pimsy was squeezing Neville's arm a bit hard. This part of the castle had always been uncomfortable and Uncle Pimsy was so close that his drool was reaching the cuff of his afternoon suit. Any closer and Pimsy might be on Neville's tie.

"Go piddle a poodle, Pimsy," said Neville. "I'm running things."

"You always were a perfect rotter," said Pimsy.

Seven

Generalissimo Moombasa waited for the American woman to be delivered. He would interrogate her himself, he decided, and he would use his wiles instead of torture.

He would show her his subtle nature, his romantic side, make her want to help the Hamidian people's struggle against imperialism or whatever.

And if that didn't work, he'd beat the information out of the American bitch.

For the first meeting, he chose the military presence of his armored corps uniform. It was robin's-egg blue with gold epaulettes, tight bands with black Cordoba leather boots, with the Hamidian insignia of a condor embossed in gold and green.

The hat was a high peak supported by the same condor insignia. In tiny zircons, the motto of the armored corps was displayed across the visor. The motto read:

"Crush the world beneath our treads."

It was a very big visor. The armored corps was 300 strong and every man had a uniform. But since the uniforms were so expensive, the People's

Democratic Republic of Hamidia had to cut back somewhere else.

So the armored corps made do with a 1948 Studebaker with an extra layer of tin on the outside, held in place by zircon studs, naturally spelling out "Crush the world beneath our treads."

A foreign manufacturer had once gotten to the armored corps and convinced its officers that they should have tanks, under the reasoning that other countries' armored corps had tanks. Many tanks. Big tanks. And with treads.

How did it look for Hamidia to have a slogan: "Crush the world beneath our treads" when it didn't even have treads, but four 1949 Firestone Silverrides, three of which were bald?

"You not only don't have treads, you don't even have traction," said the manufacturer.

"That all right, Señor. We don't have much engine either," said one of the officers. But the idea caught on and the armored corps was close to rebellion when Moombasa, being a shrewd Third World politician, recognized the meaning of the revolutionary ferment in the souls of his valiant warriors.

"Great heroes of the Hamidian revolution, I will follow your desires. We can buy a tank that only a few can use at one time, or we can buy new cravats for everyone, beige to offset the robin's-egg blue of your glorious uniforms."

There was instant outrage among the Hamidian officer corps.

"Beige don' go with robin's-egg blue. Navy blue. Black even. Maybe a dark green. But not beige."

"I am a foot soldier," said Generalissimo Moombasa. "What do I know of armored warfare and you brave men who carry it out?" And then he ordered the cravats, one of which he now wore. He realized that he could really trust his tank commanders. He ordered navy-blue cravats and found out that they were right. The navy blue really went well with the robin's-egg blue.

Moombasa was dressed when Neville Lord Wissex arrived, wearing a gray coat, top hat, white gloves. But no woman.

"Where is the woman? Where is my woman? Where is the reader of the ancient tongue of the Hamidian traders?"

"She is with her bodyguards. All the snipers you saw here last week are no more. They are dead," said Lord Wissex.

Moombasa couldn't believe his ears. The man was calm. Wissex was talking without a tremor in his voice and the man was telling him he did not have what Moombasa had paid well for.

"You failed," screamed the generalissimo.

"Yes," said Wissex.

"That's it? Yes? Just yes? Ten million dollars and you are telling me yes?"

"Yes," said Lord Wissex.

"He is telling me yes," said Moombasa to an aide. The aide nodded and offered a suggestion.

"Shoot him."

"Let's find out first why he is not afraid," said Moombasa.

"Then we shoot him," said the aide.

"Sure," said Moombasa.

"Hey, you. Brit. Where is the woman who reads

Hamidian? Where is the mountain of gold? Where the things I pay for?"

"In stronger hands than ours, your Excellency," said Wissex.

Moombasa liked the way the Briton said "your Excellency." It had class and made him feel kingly. It made him feel that perhaps he could go to Buckingham Palace, possibly even cop a feel there. If not the queen, perhaps a princess or two.

"What stronger hands?" he asked.

"Major nations against whom I would advise you not to compete," said Wissex blandly.

"Why you can't beat them? Those major nations, are they big shots?"

"We could beat them," Wissex said.

"Then why you not do it?"

"Because it would be a strain on your economy. We have to move technologically, sustain losses, advance despite those losses. I wanted to give you what a backward nation could afford."

"Hey, what you say?"

"Your Excellency?" asked Wissex.

"What you say there? That word?"

"What word?"

"Backward," said Moombasa.

"You have no industry. You have no road system or telephone system that works. No hospitals that aren't staffed by Europeans at the higher levels, no air force that works without European direction, and you produce absolutely nothing except more Hamidians."

"We produce oil and cobalt."

"Americans produce it," Wissex said. "You, I am afraid, just lay title to it because you were born here, Excellency. That is what you produce. And with the money from materials that Americans mine and drill for, you buy Americans, ambassadors, journalists, and of course the leftists whom you get for nothing. I have not forgotten your trying to pawn off Myra Waxelburg and Dudley Rawlingate III as some sort of Vanguard Revolutionary Suicide squad."

Moombasa looked at his aide. Such insults. No one called backward nations backward anymore. They emerging or developing or Third World. You didn't go to no ugly woman in the street and say you ugly. So you didn't call no Third World nations what they were either. And here was this man who took his money calling the People's Democratic Republic of Hamidia what it was.

Moombasa felt blood come up hot from his toes. He didn't want to shoot the Brit that moment because then he couldn't have the joy of killing him again. He thought of fire. Slow fire under the feet. Burn off his toenails. Put out his eyes. Peel away his chest. And the generalissimo felt himself chuckling. His aides moved away in fear. Everyone left but Neville Lord Wissex.

"So, being a backward nation, I would advise against your spending another ten million on a technological phase assault that may produce absolutely nothing. That may not even gain for you that mountain of gold which belongs to you and is worth perhaps tens of trillions of dollars."

"How many zeroes that?" asked Moombasa.

"At least twelve in your counting," said Wissex.

"Spend, you British dog," Moombasa said.

"It's too much for you to handle."

"I say spend," Moombasa said.

"Well. If you say so."

"I demand so," said Moombasa. "Demand. I will give it to you in cash. And there is more where that came from."

Moombasa was, of course, talking about his personal wealth. By now it exceeded the national treasury five-fold. But his honor had been insulted. He hardly listened to the Brit explain that the three were now in St. Maarten but would soon be in Bombay where a trap would be laid. The words about these assassins using the human body better than anyone ever had before meant nothing to him. Nothing.

"And so in ancient Bombay these ancient assassins will fall beneath the most modern of technology," Wissex said.

"And there's more where that came from," said Moombasa.

But later, when Wissex left, Moombasa reflected and decided that he would do a little work on his own. Just to protect his investment, which had now grown to $20 million.

"Bombay," said Terri Pomfret, returning from the beach on the western, the French side, of the island of St. Maarten. She noticed that Remo hadn't tanned even though he was lying out in the sun.

She set the rubbing of the Hamidian inscription on the table of their balcony facing the calm bay, under the hot white sun.

Word by word, phrase by phrase, she translated the coordinates of the sailing merchants and the descriptions of the ancient people to whose city the mountain of gold had been moved.

"In their time, this city would have to be Bombay and the people would have to be Indian and I'm certain they refer to the Temple of the goddess Gint. That was my main clue. She is the goddess of inner peace and exists only at the city limits of Bombay. Simple, You see?"

She looked around for approval, but Chiun merely continued to stare off at the horizon. Remo yawned and continued not to tan.

"Why don't you tan?" she said.

"Don't want to."

"You know, you have a basically hostile personality."

"Why not?" Remo said.

Terri did not speak to him all the way on the three different flights to India. She noticed he did not sleep much either, perhaps fifteen minutes a night.

"I suppose you won't tell me why you need so little sleep either," she said.

"I'll tell you but you won't understand," he said.

"Try me."

"I sleep more intensely. There are different levels of sleep and I sleep all of them at once. You see, with me, I am in control of body functions that you're not in control of. Tanning, everything. I can tan because I can control the element in my skin that tans. Or I can not tan."

"Ask a silly question and you get an absolutely stupid answer," said Dr. Terri Pomfet.

* * *

There were two problems with the Bombay Airport. One was that Remo, Chiun, and Terri were photographed by some lunatic wearing a Gunga Din costume, who kept sneaking around, trying not to be noticed and was therefore noticed.

The bigger problem with Bombay Airport was that it was downwind from a great concentration of Indians. It was downwind from the city and from the river it used as a refuse system for its sewage. When there was sewage. Mainly, the Indians just used the streets.

Tourist photographs of the city showed only the colors, the beautiful pastels, the fetching eyes peering out over diaphanous veils, the beautiful domed temples, the exquisitely carved nose rings, stately beige oxen walking down through the ages of man.

Photographs did not show what the oxen left behind them.

Stories never mentioned what Terri had to go through as she set foot off the plane and began retching with the other tourists who were now experiencing exciting India, moral leader of the Third World.

The tourist group's Indian guide explained how India was based on democratic principles and the highest moral values of mankind. What was even better was that the tourists didn't have to worry about pickpockets because the local police dealt with pickpockets by sticking pins in their eyes, very effectively blinding them forever.

"So we have two things. A moral order of the highest plane and safe streets."

But no one listened to the guide. Eyes teared up over handkerchiefs and people were giving up their beautiful Air India lunches which had been served with flowers. Now everyone knew why India grew such luxurious flowers.

"Plant 'em in the air and they'll be fertilized," said one tourist.

Terri looked up to Remo and Chiun who were walking along, obviously unbothered by the stench.

"How do you do it?" she gasped.

"We don't breathe as much when we don't want to," Remo said.

"Bastard," said Terri. "You joke now."

"I could help you but you are going to have to trust me."

"I'd rather vomit," said Terri.

"You make too much noise retching," said Remo, and he pressed Terri's spine and removed some of the tension in her stomach and spinal column.

"Breathe deep," he said.

"I can't."

"Yes, you can." Remo closed her nose and covered her mouth with his free hand. He let the oxygen debt build up red in her face and then released her. Terri gagged in a complete lungful of air.

She looked around startled. She waited to vomit. But suddenly the air was breathable. There was no smell to it.

"What did you do?" she asked Remo.

"I acclimated you quickly. You can't smell it because India is now a part of you. Don't breathe seeds, though, or you'll have flowers coming out of your mouth in no time."

"Well, thanks anyhow," said Terri.

In rapid-fire Korean, Chiun told Remo that one

should never expect gratitude from the pitiful because when they were relieved of their burden of stupidity, they always turned on their benefactors.

"How can you say that?" asked Remo. "That's not always the case."

"It was with you," said Chiun and he chuckled and Remo knew that Chiun's trip to India had just been made worthwhile by that single remark.

"Heh, heh, it was with you," Chiun repeated. "Heh, heh."

"Your Master of Sinanju seems so happy, it is always a pleasure to be around him," said Terri, who still could not understand the street Korean that Chiun had spoken to Remo.

Far off in a little valley they could see the pink-domed temples of the goddess Gint. Lustrous glass filled curving apertures in the many windows of the goddess' home. Poles reflecting silver and gold and emeralds glistened before the delicate jade and ivory archways.

"I don't see the mountain," said Terri.

"You will find another sign," Chiun said.

"How do you know?" asked Terri.

"Someone tried this every so often," Chiun said. "You would think they would learn." But he would explain no more.

The paving leading to the pool was inlaid with ivory upon polished marble. Pictures of the goddess Gint consorting with the god of thunder were everywhere.

A pack of the faithful stood before one of the priests. They wore rags and he wore just a loincloth and lay on his back upon a bed of sharpened spikes.

It was this proof of body control that let him

speak to the multitudes. He had not only been trained as a priest of Gint but had been to the London School of Economics, where he learned to hate America.

He also hated Britain, France, West Germany and all the Western industrialized countries. This was easy to come by in London where he had been exposed to what he and most of the other Third World students really hated about the West. They weren't part of it.

Seeing Remo and Terri, he spoke in English to the multitudes.

"Here they are. The imperialists. Why don't you have skyscrapers like they have? Because they have exploited them from you. Why don't you have as many shirts as they have? Because they have many shirts while you do not even have one. Is that fair? They consume so much of the resources of the world that you have nothing. They ride around in big cars while you walk on bare feet. Is that fair? There they are. The imperialists come to step on you."

Thus spoke the fakir dedicated to the goddess Gint. Now the beggars who stood around did not understand English but the fakir knew the talk was not for them, for they had no coins for his begging bowl. It was for the Americans themselves, because if you called Americans or Britons imperialist exploiters, they would put bills in your bowl. Especially American women who were stupid enough to believe that if Americans had fewer shirts, somehow Indians would have more.

The Britons were not as good for this, sometimes thinking things through. But American women were absolutely splendid, believing that somehow American use of bauxite and petroleum deprived people in loincloths of something they would otherwise use.

The fakir saw the American man approach. He could see that his speech had gotten to the woman but the American's man's face was hard to read.

"Exploiter of the masses, have you come to step on us? Have you come to steal our bauxite? Are you robbing us of our manganese and ferrous oxide?"

The fakir lifted his head very gently for a sudden move on his bed or nails would let the sharpened spikes pierce his backbone.

"Pig. Brutalizer. Robber," he said to Remo and Terri. Terri put fifteen dollars American into the bowl. Remo stepped up and onto the fakir, pressing him down into his nails, making sure the upper back went down with the first step so there would be no more noise out of the mouth.

The fakir lay there embedded on his spikes. Remo took back Terri's fifteen dollars and gave it to the crowd.

Terri looked at the fakir, the crowd, the fakir, Remo, and the fakir again. Already flies were settling on him.

"Why . . . what did you do that for?" she gasped.

"Listen, if he says I came to step on him, who am I to prove him wrong?"

"You're the ugly American. Absolutely," she said.

"Why not?" said Remo and the day was good.

Terri turned to Chiun. "Did you see him? He just killed a man. For no reason at all. A poor simply holy man speaking the truth as he knew it."

Chiun said nothing but Remo snapped, "I don't know what the matter is with you, but you seem to take some malignant anti-American crap and invest it with virtue. You don't know what he was talking about. Maybe he was ragging the crowd to mob us. Would you rather have seen me kill the crowd?"

"All this death all the time. Why, why, why?" asked Terri.

"Because, because, because," said Remo.

"That's not an answer."

"It is for me," Remo said.

"You beast," said Terri.

And in Korean, Chiun said to Remo about the fakir now impaled on his bed of nails, "I always wanted to do that. I always wanted to do that."

Terri did not understand what he said, but she said, "That's right, Chiun. You tell him that professional assassins don't kill wantonly."

"It seemed right," Remo said to Chiun in Korean.

"Don't listen to him," Terri said to Chiun. "He could corrupt you."

"If you see another one," Chiun said in Korean, "He's mine. I don't know why we never thought of that before."

"You've got to be special," said Remo with pride.

"I am," said Chiun. "That's why I don't know why I never thought of that before."

Suddenly Terri sobbed. "I hate you," she sputtered at Remo. "I hope the mob does mob us. How's that?"

"No. They only go after you if you look weak. They'll never attack anyone who steps a fakir into his nails," Remo said.

Terri looked. It was true. All the beggars were looking at the punctured corpse as a curiosity. No one was bothering them. One of them peeled off the corpse's loincloth to use as his own.

According to legend, the goddess Gint mated with the forces of the universe to create the god of dark places.

Gint herself was said to have murdered a part of the day which people would never see again. It was not morning or evening, but was supposed to occur shortly after noon and according to legend, was a cool and dark moment, a brief respite from the hot Indian sun.

This did Gint take into her bosom and away from mankind. Naturally, it made her one of the India's most beloved goddesses. She was widely regarded as the benefactress of schemes, and the cult of Gint was one of the richest in India.

Yet this day as Remo and Chiun accompanied Terri into the temple looking for more Hamidian writing, no one was tending the flowers or the candles or the sweetmeats set at the feet of the goddess' statue.

Gint had seven breasts and according to Indian mythology eight sons, who promptly destroyed the weakest by cutting off his lips so he could not eat.

Seeing how much more milk there was, the strongest son decided to take all the breasts for himself and when his brothers were suckling, bit off the backs of their heads. Angered, Gint ordered her remaining son never to drink her milk again but to drink the dark brackish waters in small ponds and to live forever as a mud slug.

So to that very day, devout Hindus were careful of stepping on mud lest they profane the only remaining son of Gint.

"How spiritual. How beautiful," said Terri, reading the legend under the statue and smelling the incense candles.

"The statue's got a face like a mushroom and seven tits," Remo said. "She's the ugliest thing I've ever seen."

"How beastly you are. In the presence of such spirituality, showing how gross you are."

Their footsteps sounded like coins dropping on the taut skin of a drumhead. The ceilings were painted with snakes devouring babies and slugs drinking from the breast of swamps. This was done in rubies, emeralds and sapphires.

Remo noticed little bundles taped to the ceiling where the support pillars were. Every pillar had them.

They felt wrong. He looked toward Chiun and the old Korean nodded.

"Let's find the writing and get the hell out of here," Remo said.

"It should be right near this temple," said Terri. "But I don't want to profane their religion."

"The only way you can profane it is by having an honest thought," Remo said. He looked up at the bundles and he saw Chiun nod to him. They did not belong in the temple of the goddess Gint.

Tonaka Hamamota, number one adviser to the great House of Wissex, had watched the trio enter the temple.

He had sat quite comfortably at a distance, letting his computer watch the people. It did not tell him much about their facial features, but instead how they moved and emitted heat. The heat emissions came out on a screen, showing the coolness of the temple stones and the heat of the three bodies entering.

Lord Wissex had assured him the three would enter and so they had, and that was all Tonaka Mamamota needed, since he could trail a target by the scent of the wax in their ears.

Tonaka had been told that there might be danger and that he should report every step as he did it. He thought the idea of danger was ridiculous but one did as one's employer wished.

Tonaka Hamamota wore a blue imitation cotton Sears suit with imitation silk striped tie and an imitation polyester white shirt.

He watched as his computer screen ticked off the facts:

Movement of trio. Males glide with the very motion of body. Woman clomps as is normal. Males seem always to have weight centered.

Pulse. Woman normal. Males subnormal, closer to python than ape.

Position: Males always keep female between them in protective cordon.

Language: Famale doing most of talking; apparently hostile.

First attack: Males' movement instantaneous with explosion. Female, delayed normal reaction time. Scream.

*   *   *

Terri started yelling as the tile around their feet exploded in little luminescent fragments pitting the walls with impact.

She tried to run but felt a strong reassuring hand on her arm.

It was Remo.

"There's nowhere to run," he said.

"Let me go."

"You can't run. Those are bombs going off. The whole temple's a bomb. Look." And he pointed and she followed his finger and then saw the packages strapped to the pillars where they joined the graceful dome of the roof.

She felt Remo pull her toward the ground. His finger touched an inlaid tile.

"This is a bomb too," he said. "There are nothing but bombs here. We're in the middle of a bomb."

"Oh, no," moaned Terri. She began to shake.

"It's all right, kid," Remo said. "They're not going to kill you."

"How do you know?"

"You'd have been dead by now," Remo said.

"The bombs were obvious from the beginning," Chiun said.

"Then why did we walk in here?"

"I didn't know who they were for," Chiun said. "It was obvious they were not part of the temple. Look at the strapping. Look at the packages. See how clean the lines are."

"Good taste," said Remo.

"Probably Japanese," Chiun said.

"Definitely not Indian," Remo said.

"It's in good taste," Chiun agreed.

"Definitely not Indian," Remo said.

"They're going to kill us and you're talking about design," Terri screamed.

"If we're going to die, it's not going to hurt us to talk about design."

"Do something," shouted Terri and Remo obligingly did a little tap dance and sang two bars from "Once Upon a Blue River, Darling."

Not to be outdone, Chiun recited a stanza of Ung poetry.

"That's not what I want you to do," Terri yelled.

"Name it," said Remo.

"Get us out of here," Terri said.

"We could get out but you can't," said Remo. "Look at the windows and doors. Do you see those beautiful square lattices that look like borders?"

Terri nodded.

"Bombs," said Remo. "We could get out fast enough but not you."

"You've got to protect me."

"And we are."

"Then do something," she said.

"We are," Remo said.

"You're doing nothing. You're just standing there."

"We're waiting," Remo said.

"For what?"

"For what is going to come, my dear," said Chiun and suddenly there were voices in the temple. It was one voice but because of the echoes it sounded like many. It said:

"I can kill you any time. Watch."

Suddenly Terri's ears ached from two concussions.

"That is an example," the voice said. "You are in a bomb I have constructed. Resistance is useless."

"See. I told you we were in a bomb," Remo said. "Whole place is a bomb."

"Oh, no," sobbed Terri.

"Send the woman out to me or you will all die," said the voice.

"What should I do?" whined Terri.

"You could die honorably with us," said Remo, "or you could run for your life."

"I don't want to leave you," said Terri. "But I don't want to die either."

"Then go."

"I'll stay," she said.

"No, go. Don't worry about us."

"Will you be all right?" she asked.

"Sure. Go," said Remo.

"I hate to leave you, Chiun," she said.

"Ahhh, to see beauty as one's last sight is but a pleasant way to pay the debt of death that is owed from one's birth."

"You're so beautiful," said Terri. "And you, Remo, if only you weren't so hostile."

"So long, kid," Remo said. "See you around."

Terri stumbled from the temple, holding her head, shielding her weeping eyes from the bright sun. She walked past the pools, following the sound of a voice that told her to keep moving.

The voice kept repeating that when Terri came just over the little hillock facing the temple, the two inside the temple would be released unharmed.

Terri stumbled from the temple gardens and sobbed her way beyond a little hill, where a fat Oriental with a square face, wearing a blue suit, sat in front of a little computer built into an attaché case.

"Dr. Pomfret?" he said.

"Yes."

"I have receivers in the temple that capture and magnify my voice. They are smaller than a pencil dot."

Hamamota picked up a tiny microphone, no larger than a thumbnail, and into it he spoke.

"Now you die, Melican dogs."

The temple of the goddess Gint went up in a mountain of pink plaster and spraying jewels. The earth shook. Terri felt her ears grow numb. The pink plaster of the temple was still coming down over the outskirts of Bombay when Terri finally got herself to look over the little hillock. Where Remo and Chiun had been was now only a large, smoldering hole. They were dead.

Then she thought she heard them arguing from the Beyond. The voices came through the buzzing in her ears.

"He called me an American," said Chiun.

"No. He called you a Melican," said Remo.

"That's how they pronounce American," Chiun said.

"So?"

"Would you like to be called a boy when you are a man?" said Chiun's voice from the Beyond.

"There's no comparison," said Remo's voice in Heaven.

"It is bad enough being called a Chinaman. But to be called an American. That means I have those funny eyes, that sickly skin, that awful odor about the body. It means that I am of European stock, and therefore, somehow related to the French. That is beyond degradation."

"I'm white," Terri heard Remo's voice say.

"And don't think that has been easy on me," said Chiun.

"And I am very proud to be an American," Remo said.

"Compared to being French, why not?" said Chiun.

Terri turned around. They were alive. Unscathed. And standing behind Hamamota whose eyes were open wide with amazement. He looked first at the two and then at his little computer. He punched in several commands.

The computer immediately flashed a message back. In green luminescent letters, the computer told Hamamota: "Good for you. Once again you have succeeded. The two are dead."

Froth formed on Hamamaota's lips. His face turned red. His eyes bulged. He punched new information into the computer.

The information said: "Not dead. Standing behind me."

The computer was instantaneous in its response. "Reject inaccurate information. Please check source material."

Hamamota looked behind him again.

"Alive," he punched into the machine.

The computer answered: "All input accurate until last message. Must reject."

"How did you escape alive?" asked Terri.

But Remo and Chium were not listening to her. Chiun had seen screens like that. What he wanted to know was where was the little yellow face that ate the squares and the dots. He asked Hamamota.

"Not that kind of computer," the Japanese said.

"No Pac-man?" said Remo.

"Not that kind of computer. It killed you. Why are you not dead?"

"Does it do horoscopes?" asked Remo.

"I am a Leo," said Chiun. "That's the best sign. Remo is a Virgo. He doesn't know that but I do. He couldn't help that anymore than he could help being white."

"You dead," yelled Hamamota angrily. "Why you not dead? Why you standing here?"

"Maybe it has Missile Command?" said Remo. "Where's the joystick for shooting missiles?"

"No Missile Command. This assassin computer. Best in world. Number one."

"How the world demeans glory. They have made a game of assassination. The profession of assassin is now reduced to an arcade game," Chiun said.

"You dead," yelled Hamamota.

"Does it have blackjack?" asked Remo.

"You bombed," said Hamamota. "I bombed you."

"It did work the bombs, Little Father," Remo said to Chiun.

"Still a game," Chiun said.

"Heeeeeyahhhh," yelled Hamamota and leaped into a martial arts position, hissing like an animal.

"What's that?" asked Remo.

"Another game," said Chiun in disgust.

"You die. Heeeeeeyahhhhh," screamed Hamamota, thrusting a bladelike hand toward Remo's neck.

The hand bounced back with four broken bones. The neck didn't move.

"Could I set off a bomb with that thing?" asked Remo.

"Pigs use booms," Chiun said. "Chinamen use them. They invented gunpowder because they lacked internal discipline."

Hamamota's hand hung limply by his side. His eyes bulged with hate and from his very spine, he threw a kick out at the head of the aged Korean. Chiun walked by and went to the computer inside the attaché case.

"I have seen advertisements for a boom where there is a bucket to catch the boom and that is how you score."

"I don't think this is that one, Little Father," said Remo, "because the temple really blew up."

"Maybe there are controls for catching the booms too. Does this do catching and if so, where does it score?" asked Chiun.

Hamamota lay on his side, his back thrown out of joint, his striking hand limp, exhaustion and pain on his face.

"Listen to me, fat thing," said Chiun. "Does this have a scorer? Can we blow Calcutta up from here? If we can, how many points do we get?"

"Why would you get points for blowing up Calcutta?" asked Remo.

"Have you ever seen Calcutta?"

"No," said Remo.

"Go there sometime. You would get not only points but a blessing for it. One of the truly bad places in the world," Chiun said.

"Baghdad is bad," said Remo.

"Baghdad has beauty," said Chiun.

"Baghdad has Iraqis," said Remo.

"No place is perfect," said Chiun, "except Sinanju."

"How many points for Baghdad?" Remo asked Hamamota. The Japanese wriggled onto his belly. Inch by painful inch, he crawled toward Remo and Chiun. When he got to Remo's shoes, he opened his mouth to bite and Remo lifted his foot and stepped down with one precise step, separating Hamamota into two parts.

Terri fainted.

"See if you can do Calcutta," said Remo.

"I can't do Calcutta," said Chiun.

"Why not?"

"No joystick. I think this fat Jap probably threw it away."

By the time Terri recovered, Remo and Chiun had carried her back to the temple ruins and were digging around for the Hamidian inscription.

"You didn't have to kill him," she said to Remo.

"What should I have done?"

"Rehabilitate him," said Terri.

"Right," said Chiun. "Correct." And then in Korean he said to Remo: "What is the matter with you? You would argue with a stone wall. Do you really think this woman knows what she is talking about?

"Thank you," said Terri, sure the kindly old Korean was explaining decency to his rude and crude student.

"You're welcome," said Chiun to Terri, and then to Remo: "See how easy it is when you treat idiots like idiots."

"I just want you to know this," Terri told Remo. "There has been death and destruction this day and all you could think about was playing games with human lives. You kill without remorse or even anger. I could understand anger. But nothing? Nothing? *Nothing?*"

"Would it make you feel better if I hated everybody I kill?" said Remo. "You want hate?"

"Moron," said Chiun in English.

"I don't know why you put up with him," Terri told Chiun.

"Neither do I," said Chiun.

Eight

Dr. Harold W. Smith waited in the headquarters of CURE, sitting atop staffs he could not reach, a network unconnected to anything, running dummy corporations and fronts all operating without purpose.

Through the years, he alone had set up these groups to create a network of people gathering and dispensing information, all them helping, without knowing it, to help CURE fight crime and to keep America alive.

Only Smith, each president, and CURE's lone killer arm knew what CURE was. Clerks gathering information on illegal trucking and fraud never knew for whom they really worked. Government agencies with vast sprawling budgets never knew how much of their workforce actually worked for that secret organization set up in Rye, New York, behind the facade of the sanitarium called Folcroft.

Smith had prepared for everything and he had not prepared for this. He was not even sure how long the networks would keep working or what they would do or if they would just gather, organize, penetrate, and then do it all over again because the information just wasn't being used.

He didn't know. Only the computers would know, and his computers' brains were as blank as a baby's at birth.

For the first time since those murky days when a desperate president had called on him to set up this organization, Harold W. Smith was out of touch with it all.

For the first time, there were no two dozen problems to be juggling at one time.

For the first time, there was only that blank computer terminal, with the lights flashing meaningless symbols.

And suddenly Harold W. Smith found himself doing something he had not done since grade school when he had finished reading Peter Rabbit ahead of the rest of the class. He was doodling with a pencil. He was drawing pictures.

There was a box inside a box inside a box.

He looked at it a moment and then he knew what he would do. Trying to track down the missing computer records had failed. There had been no response.

But if he set up just the sort of illegal operation that activated the CURE network? Then when it latched on to him, he could send Remo up through the network. . . .

The pencil dropped on the desk. So Remo could go up through the networks and then what? None was connected to any other and Smith was disconnected from the whole mess. He was alone and in this aging part of his life, when the body stopped responding to the commands of the mind, he was becoming useless.

And then the telephone rang.

It was the technician in the new headquarters in St. Maarten. They had received a strange message several days after the failed transmission from someone. Would Smith be interested?

"Absolutely. I want to know everything about the message, especially where it originates," said Smith.

"I'm sorry, sir, but we didn't get that. Just somewhere in the western part of your country."

"All right. What does it say?" Smith asked.

"It says 'Offer interesting. Will only deal gross.' "

"Deal gross?"

"That's it, sir."

"Did the sender mean big or large or ugly or what?" Smith asked.

"I don't know. Only deal gross, it says."

"Who will only deal gross?"

"He didn't send the message properly," the technician said. "We didn't get a name or frequency or anything."

"All right. We're going to transmit again."

"During a storm again, sir?"

"No. Continuously. Around the clock," said Smith. "Sun and rain, storm and clear. Sent it all over."

"I certainly hope the stockholders of Analogue Networking Inc. don't find about this, sir," said the technician.

"Why should they?" asked Smith. What was this? Some kind of blackmail?

"It would just be terribly costly," the technician said.

"That's right. And I'm telling you to do it and don't you worry about the stockholders," Smith said. "That is not your concern. You understand?"

"Yes sir," the man said.

"Just do it," Smith said.

In Beverly Hills, Barry Schweid informed Bindle and Marmelstein that he had found a producer who would give him a percentage of the gross profits. He was taking all his screenplays to the other producer.

So Hank Bindle and Bruce Marmelstein called an urgent meeting. If there were a producer out there willing to give gross points, that meant he was sure the screenplay was dynamite. He was sure it would make money.

Therefore, the screenplay was good. But which screenplay? There had been a half-dozen. Bindle and Marmelstein owned four Schweid treatments.

Was it the dynamite box-office blockbuster?" asked Marmelstein.

"No, I don't think so. The dynamite box-office blockbuster was so boring people fell asleep when they read the title."

"What about the new-wave film that was going to bury all the other producers?" asked Bruce Marmelstein.

"Nobody could understand that," said Hank Bindle.

"The assassin thing?" said Marmelstein.

"Right," said Bindle. "I bet that thieving producer wants the assassin thing."

"We don't own the assassin thing," Marmelstein wailed. "That was the screenplay we didn't buy."

"Why not?"

"We didn't have anyone to read it," said Marmelstein.

"Where was the creative director?"

"She quit when she found out she was getting less than the secretaries."

"What about the secretaries?" asked Bindle. "Couldn't they read it to you?"

"It came in on a Saturday."

"So you just rejected it?" said Hank Bindle, angered.

"Why not? It looked like any other Schweid script to me. How should I know it was a good script? There wasn't a picture in it."

"What do you mean, picture? You mean you can't read?" said Hank. He stood up from the table. "I have been beating my buns off for months now trying to get a picture off the ground and now my partner tells me he can't read."

"Why didn't you read it?" said Bruce. "You could have read it."

"I was giving meetings."

"You could have read it. It wasn't long. It was less than half an inch thick. Read it now," said Bruce, bringing a carton of manuscripts from behind a large marble statue of a girl holding a lamp of wisdom.

"Okay," said Hank. "I'll have it read by midnight. Give it to me."

"What do you mean, give it to you?" said Bruce, his neck jewelry clanking with rage.

"Give me the script and it'll be read by morning."

Marmelstein reached into the box. There were three scripts about a half-inch thick each.

"It's one of these," he said. "The epics are three-quarters of an inch."

"Do I have to take all three?" asked Hank Bindle.

"No. Just the assassin one."

"Is that the one with the coffee spot on it?"

"You can't read either," screamed Marmelstein.

"I used to. I just don't need it anymore. If I could read, I'd be a publisher, not a producer. I used to read beautifully. Everybody said so."

"So did I," said Bruce.

"Why did you stop?" asked Hank.

"I don't know. You don't use something, you forget how," said Bruce.

"I can still recognize my name in print," said Hank Bindle.

"I can too," said Bruce Marmelstein. "It's got a lot of round bumpy letters in it."

"Mine has got curls," said Hank Bindle.

Nine

Chiun had wandered off when Remo grabbed Terri by the arm and growled, "Come on. You've marched us all over every depressing place in the world. We're getting out of here. Another day in this dump and I'll have rickets and morality and an undying affection for cows."

They picked their way slowly over the lumps of marble and stone and in the distance saw Chiun's tiny figure, swathed in his brocaded kimono, standing near the rubble of the temple, looking down at something.

The beggars who lined the pool to the now-destroyed temple had already begun to drift back, taking their accustomed begging spots.

"What's he doing?" Terri asked Remo, looking toward Chiun.

"He likes to pose," Remo said. "Looks like he's doing something significant."

"He must be doing *something*."

"Suit yourself. Go see." Remo freed Terri's arm and she walked quickly down along the length of the pool toward Chiun.

A beggar approached Remo. One eye was rolled back into his head and there was dried spittle along the right side of his mouth.

"Beg pardon, American friend. Do you have a dollar for a poor but honest beggar?"

"No."

"Half a dollar?"

"No."

"Anything . . . any alms?"

"Here's a dime," Remo said. "Go buy yourself a cabinet ministry."

He flipped the beggar a coin, and saw Terri drop to her knees next to Chiun in the temple wreckage, and begin to smooth away debris with her hands. Casually, Remo strolled along the pool toward them.

When he joined them, he said, "Oh, jeez, not another one."

"Shhh," Terri said. She was tracing her fingers over a gold plaque, following the lines of the peculiar wedge-shaped letters that had been chiseled into the soft metal. The plaque was now curled up at both ends, like a piece of fresh lettuce.

Remo guessed that the plaque had been buried somewhere under the temple and had been blown to the surface by the force of the explosion.

"I don't care what it says," Remo said. "We're going home."

"We'll go where it takes us," Terri snapped. "Be quiet. This is important."

Chiun looked toward Remo and shook his head as if Remo should not waste his time arguing with an imbecile. Remo nodded.

He picked up a handful of smooth stones from

the rubble and amused himself by tossing them at the beggars who were again lined along the low wall facing the pool. He put fourteen stones in a row into fourteen different tin cups. Every time one of the stones landed in a cup, the beggar would pull the cup to his body, shield it with his arms from the other beggars, and peer inside to see what godly gift he had been sent. Not one of the beggars showed any interest in the destruction of the old temple or even came up to look. Nor had the police showed up. Did India have police? Remo wondered. The country had a hundred thousand gods, but did it have any police? How could you govern a country that had more gods than police?

Terri stood up after ten long minutes.

"Spain," she said. "The gold went to Spain."

"And then to the Bronx," Remo said in disgust.

"It says Spain," she said stubbornly.

"You find this writing acceptable?" Chiun asked Terri.

"Yes," she said. "Ancient Hamidian script." She paused, then asked, "What do you mean?"

"Nothing," Chiun said and turned away.

Terri looked at Remo quizzically, but Remo said, "Don't ask me. You two are the big language mavens. I'm just along for the ride."

"I've noticed," Terri said.

Generalissimo Moombasa received Lord Wissex in his master bedroom suite, in which a bevy of naked blonde voluptuous beauties would have seemed as unnecessary as another harmonica player at a hillbilly convention. Moombasa obviously had no room in his life to love anyone but himself.

The walls of the bedroom were made of what might have been imported marble, but it was hard to tell because they were covered, almost every square inch, with mural-sized pictures of Moombasa greeting his subjects. In the small corners where the walls met, and the murals didn't totally mesh, there were smaller photos of Moombasa. Some men like mirrors over their beds, but Moombasa had another enormous mural there, the same size as his big bed, so that his last view at night, before shutting his eyes, was his own smiling face.

Moombasa was sitting up in bed, propped up by pillows, eating soft-boiled eggs from a cup. The runny albumen seemed intent on escaping his spoon and kept dribbling down onto the front of his blue velvet smoking jacket, which had gold-fringed military epaulettes on the shoulders.

Wissex was amused to note that Moombasa ate with a golden spoon from a golden egg cup. In Wissex Castle, where servants had been feeding noblemen since the days when Moombasa's ancestors were eating their own children, they used simple sterling and old china.

Albumen and yolk running down his chin, Moombasa asked, "What success?"

"None. We have failed. All is over."

The gold spoon again stopped halfway to Moombasa's mouth. Its slimy cargo puckered up against one edge, held there by surface tension, and then, as Wissex watched, the spoon tipped more and the weight of the slime exceeded its cohesion and more egg slid off the spoon's bowl onto Moombasa's chest. He ignored it.

"What?"

"It is true, Generalissimo. We have failed. The United States has won again, crushing under its militarist heel your worthwhile ambitions to rescue your people from poverty and its oppression."

"Hell with that crap. What about the gold?"

The spoon was forgotten now and its contents just kept dribbling off onto Moombasa's velvet jacket.

"I'm sorry, great leader," said Wissex. "But the House of Wissex is withdrawing. We have been at this for centuries and perhaps it is time now to close down our operations. Perhaps we will raise bees." Wissex could smell the eggs now.

Moombasa's heart went out to Wissex. He had never seen the Englishman looking and sounding so depressed. "But training. Special squads. All the things I count on you for," he said. "What of them?"

"You will have to have your own men take charge," Wissex said.

"My own men couldn't take charge of a shoeshine stand," Moombasa said. "Not if somebody gave them a picture of feet. I need you. What has happened?"

"The woman and the two bodyguards have escaped again. They have foiled the efforts of my best men."

"And you have none of these best men left?" Moombasa asked.

"We have many," Wissex said. "Our best operative is still available, but he planned on retiring several months ago. I didn't want to disturb him in his retirement, particularly on such a difficult mission."

"Disturb him," Moombasa ordered with a bellow. "You have obligation to provide me with your best. Perform this mission. That mountain of gold must be mine."

"*And* Hamidia's," Wissex corrected.

"Yes. Hamidia's. Of course," Moombasa said. "Nothing must stand in the way of the gold being returned to its rightful owner. Me. And Hamidia."

He threw the egg plate and the spoon and the tray holding them to one side. It all teetered on the edge of the bed for a moment, then fell over, smearing itself on the expensive Persian carpet. Moombasa arose, walked to Wissex, and put an arm around the Englishman's shoulders. Wissex moved slightly in his chair so that none of the egg all over Moombasa would drip on his tweed suit.

"We have been together a long time, Lord of Wissex," said Moombasa. "Now, at the pinnacle of our adventures together, is no time to stop. You use all the resources of Wissex. Together, we conquer the evil fascist Yankee beast."

"Well, if you insist . . ."

"I insist, I insist."

"I'll get on it right away," Wissex said. He rose quickly, turning away from Moombasa to protect his suit, and walked toward the door.

He went out without looking back. Moombasa looked at the closing door, pleased that he had been able to buck up Wissex's courage. A productive House of Wissex was important for his continuing rule. He thought how strange it was. People always thought of Englishmen as cool, not given to worry or panic, but here was Wissex, a very old title, coming to him, Generalissimo Moombasa, for encouragement. Someday it would be a chapter in his memoirs. How he had come to the rescue of the British lion and given him the courage of Moombasa, when the Englishman was on the verge of losing all his faculties.

Wissex reappeared in the doorway and Moombasa's eyebrows lifted in surprise.

"The same fee system?" Wissex said.

"Of course," Moombasa said grandly, with a smile. Wissex nodded and left. Just like a child, Moombasa thought. Wissex needed to be led. Just like a child.

He smiled to himself and then looked around to see if his egg had suffered so much damage on contact with the carpet as to render it uneatable.

"Commander Spencer here." The voice crackled over the long-distance telephone line.

"Wissex. Put on your scrambler."

Neville Lord Wissex waited at the Hamidia airport in the last of a bank of telephone booths. He knew that all the telephones in Hamidia were tapped because the House of Wissex had set up the procedures itself. The very best equipment in the world, Wissex had told Moombasa, when he sold him the surplus British Army World War II devices. Moombasa had insisted also on buying scrambler decoding equipment and Wissex had been happy to sell.

But the scrambler he now attached to the earpiece and mouthpiece of the telephone could not be decoded by Moombasa's expensive toys. Wissex could barely restrain a smile. Who in Hamidia had anything to say worth tapping?

But Moombasa had insisted on all the equipment when Wissex told him that the United States routinely tapped all the telephones in its country. The generalissimo had the mind of a child.

Spencer's voice came back onto the line, crackled and distorted through electronics.

"Got it, Neville," he said. "How goes it?"

"I just left the idiot. In for a penny, in for a pound."

"Good," said Spencer. "I thought you might have a spot of trouble this time."

"Not really. He's an infant. I had him ordering me to continue the battle against the American oppressors," Wissex said.

"So, what's next, old bean?"

"Well, honestly Spencer, I'm a little annoyed at this woman. *And* her two bodyguards. I thought you should take a run at them. Bring in the girl and dispose of those other two for good."

"I thought you'd never ask, old chap."

"It's just that I've had enough of wogs and hired help," Wissex said. "It's time to send a Brit. A real Brit. To do a Brit's work."

"I'll bring their heads back on my shield," Spencer said. "Where will I find them?"

"I've sent them to Spain next."

"Ahhhh, the land of señoritas and olé. Did I ever tell you about——"

Wissex knew Spencer was about to launch into one of the interminable stories of his former career as Britain's top spy. And he had heard all the stories over and over again, so he said quickly: "No, I don't think so. But later. I've got a line of baboons standing around, waiting to use this phone. Wouldn't do for them to notice the scrambler."

"Got you, old man. Next time."

"Yes. We'll talk," Wissex said.

Ten

Only the ocean hadn't changed.

That unusually philosophical thought occurred to Dr. Harold W. Smith as he sat in the semi-darkened office at Folcroft Sanitarium, looking out through the one-way glass of his windows at the Long Island Sound, pitching and surging at the end of the long green manicured lawn that dribbled down to the narrow sliver of beach.

He had changed. He had come to CURE and its first director, picked by a president he didn't like for a job he didn't want, and he took it only because the president had told him that he was the only man in the nation who could handle it. Smith then had still been young—ready to retire from the CIA after twenty years of service to his country and ready to go back to teach law in New England. The law had been his first love.

And suddenly he had been made the greatest law-breaker in the history of the United States. It was CURE's mission: to work outside the law to capture the lawbreakers; to use criminal methods to stop crime from overrunning the United States.

Smith knew of only one way to work. He had thrown himself into the assignment with the same rockhard New England tenacity he had brought to everything in his life. His marriage, never very exciting to begin with, had slowly slipped away into an arm's length exercise in boredom. He had lost touch with his young daughter and she had fallen away into the sink of drug addiction.

And CURE hadn't worked. It had struggled and carved out many successes, but it had all amounted to trying to bail out the ocean with a spoon. No matter how hard you bailed, there was even more water to take the place of whatever you removed. So too with crime. In the United States, it had become almost infinite in its scope and as it had grown more successful, it had enticed more and more people into the criminal life. In recruiting, nothing succeeds like success.

So, almost against his will, Smith had found it necessary to take CURE one step further. He had recruited a killing arm. Remo Williams, a Newark, New Jersey policeman, who had killed in Vietnam. Remo had been surly and felt abused at having his comfortable life disrupted. He had not wanted anything to do with CURE. But he had been the right man. An orphan with no family. A man who loved his country and had killed for it. Smith knew he had chosen correctly: that Remo would kill again for his country.

And he had . . . hundreds of times, now beyond count. Maybe they were still trying to spoon out the ocean but in Remo, CURE now had a bigger spoon and those whom Remo visited did not live to be criminals again.

But only the ocean had not changed.

Remo had changed. He had started out reluctantly, doing CURE's work because America needed it. But then had come the change. He had started to do the work because he was an assassin and assassin's work defined him and made him whole. Remo's sense that CURE could make a difference was long gone. There were still residues of his patriotism but they were thinner, more nebulous now than they had ever been. Remo now killed because he killed, and America was better to kill for than anybody else he could think of at the moment.

Chiun had changed too. He had been brought to CURE just to train Remo, to teach him to kill and to survive. It had started for the old Korean as just another job, but that had not lasted long.

Somewhere along the way, Chiun had decided that Remo was not just a student, but that he was to be Chiun's successor as the next Master of Sinanju. Chiun had also decided that Remo was the reincarnation of the Hindu god, Shiva the Destroyer. Smith had never really understood what Chiun was talking about. It was enough for Smith to know that Remo and Chiun were different from other men; that their minds worked differently and their bodies worked differently. Smith had never expected, and now never understood, the strange powers they would have and why they were so much more than other men.

Chiun once had explained that the only secret of Sinanju was to teach men to use all their powers; to emulate the insects who could leap scores of times their own height and lift hundreds of times their own weight. He cited the case of the shark and its senses which could detect one part of blood in a million parts of water. This, Chiun had said, was the potential that man could live up to. Smith didn't believe it. There had been nothing like that in the human physiology courses he had taken at Dartmouth. But he had seen those powers too many times now to disbelieve them.

Still, since he could neither disbelieve nor understand, he chose to ignore, and just to be thankful that those powers, whatever exactly they were, were arrayed on the side of the United States and not against it.

So they had come a long way, Smith and Remo and Chiun and CURE and America itself, and the only thing that had not changed was the water that ran back and forth endlessly in front of Smith's windows.

The telephone rang, its sharp jangle seeming visibly to jolt the quiet waves of air in the darkened room.

That was another thing that didn't change: the telephone. It had started ringing all those years before when Smith had first moved CURE into Folcroft. And it was still ringing.

He lifted the receiver slowly and said, "Hello."

Smith had never before heard the voice, which said, "What kind of deal are you offering?"

"Depends on what you've got," Smith said noncommitally. "Suppose you tell me something about yourself."

"What I've got is one of the great stories of our time. A secret agency for the United States government. An official government assassin and his elderly Oriental trainer. A father-son love theme that runs through it. Their battles against evil to try to make America safe for all its people again."

As the intense voice of Barry Schweid ranted on, Smith's stomach sank. This man, whoever he was, knew everything. CURE had been compromised.

There was silence on the end of the phone and Smith realized he was supposed to say something.

"Sounds interesting," he said. "What'd you say your name was?"

"I don't want to tell you my name," Schweid said. "Out here, they rip off everything. I don't want anybody to know what I'm working on."

Out here? Where? Smith wondered. Who rips off everything? What was this lunatic talking about?

"Like you. Like you got a message into my computer and processor," Schweid said. "I don't know how you did that. Maybe somebody else could do it. Then everybody would have everything I was working on."

His voice seemed to be approaching hysteria and Smith wondered if talking about money might calm him down.

"What kind of deal did you have in mind?" Smith said.

"I wouldn't take less than 250 thou. And ten points."

"Oh, yes, points," Smith said, totally confused. "Have to have points."

"And not net points either. Gross points. Net sucks."

"Well, that should be no problem," Smith said. No, there would be no problem. This madman, whoever he was, was due a visit from Remo. *If* Smith got his records back. *If* CURE survived that long. "We should get together and work out the details," Smith said.

"Who do you have to talk to first?" Schweid asked.

"No one. I'm in this alone."

"You're not going to make this one, are you?" Schweid asked. His voice took on a whiny, suspicious sound.

"Why not?" Smith asked. What was this man talking about?

"Nobody makes one on their own. Nobody makes a decision on their own. You've got to talk to your people. I know that. And you've got to kick it around with the creative folks. I know the bars they hang out in. Anybody who says he doesn't have to talk to anybody is lying. You're just in this to jerk me around, aren't you?"

Smith was afraid the man would hang up and he quickly said, "No, no, no. I'm a one-man operation. I make all the money decisions myself. And I handle creative myself." What the hell was he talking about, Smith wondered.

"What have you done?" Barry Schweid asked.

"A lot of things," Smith answered slowly.

"Tell me about some of them," Schweid said.

"I think we ought to swap résumés when we meet. I don't know anything about you either." Smith tried to chuckle. The unaccustomed sound resounded through the dark office like a death rattle. "Why, I don't even know your name. Maybe you're the one who can't make a deal on your own."

"No? No? You think that, huh? Well, this is mine. Totally mine. Those assholes, Bindle and Marmelstein, didn't want it. So that's their loss. I've got the property to sell."

Property? What property? Smith wonder. He wondered. He said, "I don't buy property without seeing it."

"How do I know you won't steal it from me?"

"It's hard to steal property," Smith said. How did you steal property? Did you take it with you and leave a hole in the ground where the property used to be? What was this man talking about? He wished his computers were working. He could have been running this conversation through them and by now the computer would know who this man was and where his phone was located and it would have been able to figure out, by cross-checking against lists of occupational jargon and slang, what he was talking about. But Smith's computer capabilities were down to almost zero, lost in a storm at sea. And this nuthouse lunatic had found them.

"I've had a lot of property stolen from me. Every time I pitch an idea, I see it under somebody else's name." Barry Schweid paused. "Listen, I don't want to sound tough. I want to make this deal. It's just that I've been burned."

"You won't be burned by me," Smith said. "When can we meet?"

"You say two hundred and fifty thousand is okay and ten points gross?"

"That's right," Smith said agreeably.

"I've got to think about it."

"Why? That's what you asked for. I agreed. What do you have to think about?" Smith asked.

"That's just it. You agreed. Out here, nobody agrees. You at this phone number regularly?"

"Yes."

"I'll get back to you."

The telephone clicked dead in Smith's ear. He replaced the receiver slowly, then dialed a three-digit number that connected him with Folcroft's switchboard. During the day, he had tried to start rebuilding the sanitarium's computer capability. Now he would see if there was anything happening inside the computers.

After a few seconds, the computer terminal on his desk lit up, and slowly spelled out a message.

Unable to find Telephone number. Call originated in western United States.

Smith stared at the message, then pressed a button clearing the screen.

He took out a pad and pencil and hunched over his desk to try to recreate his entire conversation with the madman. Perhaps he would be able to figure out what it was all about. He allowed himself a sigh. It was going to be another long night.

Eleven

The long oak table occupied a long narrow room, with high vaulted ceilings and intricate hand-carved wooden moldings, but both room and table were overwhelmed by a giant crest, a full six feet across that occupied the center of one wall behind the head of the table.

In the center of the brilliantly polished ceramic crest, a lion reared on its hind legs. At one side of the lion was a sheaf of wheat and on the other side, a stiletto with a diamond-studded hilt.

A ceramic sash looped across the bottom of the crest. It contained the single word: Wissex.

There were not other paintings in the room, no photographs, no wall decorations, nothing but the crest. Around the table were placed a dozen hard-seated, straight-backed chairs. A single black telephone sat on the table.

Six men were talking softly in the room, but they became silent when the door opened and Neville walked in. He wore a herringbone tweed jacket with leather elbow patches, knickers, high socks and heavy walking shoes. He gave off the scent of out-of-doors and spent shotgun shells as he breezed inside the room and walked to the head of the table.

"Everyone here?" he called out, then sat down, looked around, nodded, and said, "Good. Let's get started."

Wissex waited until the other men were seated, then tapped on the table with the end of a silver pen he kept in his inside jacket pocket. He said briskly, "The monthly meeting of the House of Wissex will come to order. The minutes and the treasurer's report will wait until the next monthly meeting. I'd like to report on the Hamidian operation."

He looked around as if inviting approval and five of the six men at the table nodded. The sixth was Uncle Pimsy. He was trying to screw his monocle into his eye, so that he could see clearly the cigar he was fondling in his hand.

Wissex waited for the old man to speak, but he said nothing. Wissex began his report. "The Hamidian operation is proceeding nicely. We have already squeezed Moombasa for twenty million. Our goal was twenty-five million and I expect to meet that goal."

"But we've incurred losses," one of the directors said. He was a red-faced man in his early thirties whose voice seemed on the verge of cracking. His principal distinguishing characteristic was an adam's apple that bobbed up and down, seemingly out of synchrony with his speech.

"Yes, Bentley," Wissex agreed easily. "We've had losses."

"How many, Neville?" the young man asked.

"Eighteen. Seven in America and ten in the Yucatan. And we just lost our bomber in Bombay."

"Why?" Bentley asked. The other directors nodded, all but Pimsy, who seemed to be trying to sculpt his cigar to fit into a one-in-a-million mouth. He was tearing at the stem of the cigar with a silver knife, grunting under his breath.

Wissex waited until the directors stopped nodding.

"I don't know," he said. "The woman is protected by just two men but somehow they have repelled our subcontractors."

"Where do they go next?" another director asked.

"Spain."

"And then where?"

"There is no other place," Wissex said. "They weren't even supposed to get this far."

"Well, we just have to get rid of those bodyguards," another director said. He was a bristly man in his forties with a battalion-grade rust mustache. "Just can't have people running around killing our field hands. Not good form, don't you know?"

"No. No. True." Voices grunted around the table.

"We *will* get rid of them," Wissex said coldly.

"Ehhhhhhhhhhhhhhhh."

The sound came from Uncle Pimsy at the end of the table. He had the cigar in his mouth now, still unlit, but the monocle had dropped again from his eye and he was trying to screw it back in.

He took a deep breath and began to speak again.

"Ehhhhhhhhhhhhhhhh." It was a terminal rattle, but the men around the table waited for him to go on. They were used to his way of starting to talk.

Finally, Pimsy pulled the cigar from his mouth and said, "Can't get rid of those two. Can't. Don't you understand?" He voice was gravelly and the words came out sounding as if his lips had been frozen with novocaine and were unable to form letters correctly. Spittle flew from his mouth with the words and the directors nearest him leaned away.

Wissex said, "That's nonsense, Uncle Pimsy, and you know it."

"Ehhhhhhhhhhhh," came the rattle again. "Tell them the truth, Neville. We're all going to die."

"Oh, come," said Neville. He looked around the table, smiling patronizingly. "Uncle Pimsy has the idea that these assassins are somehow indestructible. From the Orient. He wants us to pay them a tribute, if you can believe that."

The other directors looked first at Wissex, then at Pimsy. The old man had lighted his cigar. It filled the room with smoke as if it were a tubular tear-gas canister.

"Never liked the idea of stealing money from Moombooger," Pimsy said. "Go back to the good old days. Honest men doing honest work. You're ruining this house, Neville."

"By bringing in twenty million dollars?" he asked.

"By making us battle the House of Sinanju," Pimsy said.

"Times change," Wissex said quickly.

"Sinanju never changes," Pimsy said. "Ehhhhhhhhh."

"What is Sinanju?" asked the director named Bentley.

"Another old house of assassins," Neville said.

"Far as I can tell, it's been out of business for years. But Uncle's worried about it. Seems we met up once some hundreds of years ago and had some trouble with them. Uncle wants us to give the money back and strike our tents and go open cheese and tea shops." Anybody else want to do that besides Pimsy?"

He looked around the table. The directors were shaking their heads.

Pimsy groaned again. His monocle fell from his eye. He slumped back in his seat, as if exhausted from the effort of speaking. He puffed hard on his cigar and the smelly smoke hung in the air, a tangible fog.

"You're too clever by half, Neville. But you're going to kill all these people before you're done," Pimsy said.

"Shouldn't you go play with your poodle?" Neville snapped.

"Get rid of those bodyguards," Bentley said. "That should satisfy everybody."

"You're right," said Wissex "We concur. We will finish them off immediately. We will send our second best."

"Why *second* best?" asked Bentley.

"Because *I* have an appointment to ride to hounds this weekend. But no more foreign mongrels on this job. We will send Spencer."

"Spencer," one of the men hissed.

"Yes," said Wissex. "Commander Spencer."

There were murmurs of agreement around the table, and Wissex stood, signaling that the meeting was at an end. The others rose, still grinning and nodding to themselves.

"Oh, yes, Spencer," one of them said.

Uncle Pimsy alone remained in his seat, his chin sunk down onto what used to be his chest before his chest went south into his stomach cavity.

He was shaking his head.

"We're all going to die," he said.

Mrs. Cholmondley Montague was on her hands and knees in the garden, plucking weeds from among her flowers, when she heard the sound. It sounded as if hell had sprung a leak, a whining, screeching sound, and she closed her eyes for a moment, praying that it was an illusion and there wasn't really any such sound; but the sound continued and got louder and louder.

It had long since been arranged among the neighbors that the first to hear the sound would alert all the others, for their mutual protection, so Mrs. Montague dropped her garden tools and ran inside the house.

She looked at the telephone, her British sense of duty pulling her toward it. But self-preservation came first and so she closed and locked her front door and windows before she picked up the phone.

From a list alongside the instrument, she started calling her neighbors.

"Yes. The bagpipes. He's started up again."

"Yes. He's started. Stay inside."

She even called that terrible woman who said her name was Mrs. Wilson, but God knew, she was probably an Italian or worse, a dark thing she was and hairy, but even hairy and dark, she deserved a warning.

Still, Mrs. Montague had trouble keeping the chill out of her voice.

"I know this is the first time for you, so stay inside. I'll let you know when it's safe to come out. You can light a candle or do whatever it is your type of person does."

Soon, the quiet, dead-ended little mews was still. Only the sound of bagpipes hovered overhead. The houses looked as if they had been designed to keep out all light and air. Every door was bolted shut and every window tightly closed. Shades, Venetian blinds, drapes were pulled tight, as if the sun were a deadly bacteria-carrying enemy. Within moments, the neighborhood resembled one of those everybody-dead-by-occult-intervention neighborhoods from a Hollywood horror movie—still and unmoving as death, with only the eerie sound of the bagpipes hanging over all.

The bagpipe music came from inside a small house at the very end of the immaculate little street. Inside, playing on a stereo system, was a record of the British Black Watch Regiment. Atop that record, awaiting their turns, were a stack of records including Wagner, military music from the Boer War, military music from the Indian campaigns, and songs of the Empire.

Commander Hilton Marmaduke Spencer, O.G., K.L.M., D.S.C., sat finishing his Stolichnaya vodka neat. He could feel the throbbing in his temples, the throbbing that always signaled that he would soon kill again.

He finished off his drink, strode to a bookcase in a corner of the living room, and reached behind a slim copy of *Italian War Heroes* to press a button.

Noiselessly, the bookcase slid into the room, opening like a door to display another small room. Its walls were lined with weapons, handguns and rifles and automatic pistols. There were hand grenades and small one-man rockets, all neatly labeled and stored for immediate use.

Commander Spencer decided he would take a lot of equipment with him and give those two bloody bodyguards a really rousing sendoff.

His temples kept throbbing and he knew the pain would not subside until he was packed and ready to go on his mission. Until that time, he hoped he met no one. He hoped no neighbors were on the street and he hoped no mailmen or deliverymen came to the front door, because while the temples pounded, he was not in control of himself. And he didn't want to kill anybody right now. Not yet. Not until he had met these two bodyguards.

Twelve

At least at Kennedy Airport in New York, they had predictable hookers and muggers. But here, in the Bombay Airport, they had beggars and cows milling around the main passenger terminal.

"Ridiculous," Remo said. "This country's never going to make it into the twentieth century. Hell, it might not even make the nineteenth."

"You just don't understand spirituality," Terri Pomfret said.

"I understand cowshit," Remo said. "You're standing in it."

Terri looked down, saw she indeed was and tried to shake it from her shoe.

"Pray it off," Remo said. "Flash a buck and you'll have a thousand gurus over here to help you."

"You're back to being nasty," Terri said.

"Something about this country brings out the beast in me," Remo said.

He strolled off, picking his way through the cowchips, toward a bank of telephone booths on the far side of the terminal.

The first seven phones had dial tones but no sign of sentient life on the other end of the line. When Remo picked up the receiver on the eighth phone, an operator answered him instantly.

He gave her the 800-area-code number in the United States.

"That is wonderful," the operator said.

"What is?"

"That you're calling America. I've never placed a call to America. Are you American?"

"Will it help me get my call through if I tell you yes?" Remo asked.

"You don't have to be sarcastic. No wonder you Americans are hated around the world."

Remo began to sing:

> "In the good old colony days,
> when we lived under the king,
> lived a butcher and a baker
> and a little tailor . . . bring back
> the British."

"Vietnam," the operator yelled. "El Salvador."

"Cowshit. Dirt," Remo yelled back.

"Racism. Colonialism," the operator yelled.

"Please," Remo said, surrendering. "Just get my number."

He leaned against the wall and waited. He noticed a slight dark man, wearing a diaper around his midsection and a terrycloth turban, standing against the wall near the telephones, trying very hard not to be involved with Remo, trying very hard not to look in Remo's direction, trying very hard not to be noticed. He had a small bale of cotton alongside him. He picked it up and placed it on his head, moved a few steps along the wall, closer to Remo, then put the bale down on the floor again.

After a lot of clicking, Smith's voice came on the phone. The operator said, "Imperialist pig calling you."

She clicked the phone loudly in Remo's ear as she got off the line.

"It's Remo. We're going to Spain. Right, Smitty, Spain. Don't ask me. She says Spain, we go to Spain. You're the one who told me to do this. I know. The world depends on it. Right, right, right, right, right."

After Remo hung up, he walked over to the man in the turban and diaper who had just replaced the cotton bale on his head. Remo rearranged it even more with a quick stroke of his hand, slamming the bale down around the man's ears so he looked like a walking sofa cushion.

"We're going to Spain," Remo said. "Just ask. It's not polite to eavesdrop."

They were the only people in the plane's first-class section and Chiun took his usual seat by the window so that he could concentrate on the wing and make sure it wasn't falling off.

While the plane was taxiing, he said, "You did well, Remo."

Remo and Terri were sitting across the aisle.

"Oh, how's that?" asked Remo.

"By not getting us on an Air India plane. I would not fly anything manipulated by these savages," Chiun said.

"My honor," Remo said.

Chiun nodded and turned back to the wing.

"How can he be so nice sometimes and so mean other times?" Terri asked Remo.

"You think he's bad now?" said Remo. "Wait until you learn street Korean and find out what he's been saying behind your back."

When the plane was airborne, a stewardess came from behind the galley wall and looked over the first-class section.

When she saw Remo, she reached a hand up and opened two more buttons on her blouse. She was a tall brunette, long-legged and slim, and her candy-striped blouse was pulled tight over a full bosom.

"That stewardess is looking at you." Terri sniffed at Remo.

"Probably she's just trying to see to the end of her chest. Quite a set of chest, actually," Remo said.

"If you like cows," Terri said.

"For two days, you've been telling me to love cows. Now, all of a sudden, something's wrong with cows?"

"You're disgusting," Terri said.

The stewardess came to their seat and leaned forward over Remo's aisle seat so he could see into the dark valley of her cleavage.

"Can I get you anything, sir? Anything at all?"

"I'll have tea," Terri said.

The stewardess ignored her. "Sir? Anything?" she asked Remo again.

"No thank you," Remo said.

"Tea," said Terri.

"Oh, come on," the stewardess told Remo. "There must be something you want. Maybe you'd like to see the galley where we fix meals. It's just up there. Come on. I'll show it to you." She took Remo's hand but he extricated himself from her grip.

"No, that's all right," he said, smiling at her.

"The washroom," she said. "You'd like to inspect the washroom. Come on." She took his hand again. "I'll show the washroom to you. Show you how the door locks."

"No, thank you," said Remo.

"Tea," said Terri.

"Come on," the stewardess said. "There's got to be something you want." She leaned over farther, exposing more of her bosom. Terri turned away and looked out the window in disgust.

"Something. Anything. I'll get you a pillow."

The stewardess reached into the overhead compartment, standing on tiptoe and pressing her belly against the side of Remo's face as she rooted around in the overhead luggage section. Remo turned to Terri and shrugged helplessly. Terri stuck out her tongue.

The stewardess slipped the pillow behind Remo's head.

"It's a nice pillow. Not as nice as the ones I have in my apartment, but all right. You should try the ones in my apartment. It's all right. My roommate's out of town."

Remo said, "Thank you. Maybe some other time."

Terri said, "Tea."

"The stewardess said, "Here, let me brush those crumbs off your lap."

"I don't have any crumbs on my lap."

"I'm sure I saw some. Right there."

The stewardess brushed Remo's lap.

Remo sighed and reached behind the young brunette, placing his hand on her back, feeling the vertebrae of her spine.

"It think it's the fifth," he mumbled to himself. "Fifth or sixth. Chiun. Is it fifth or sixth?" he called out, as the stewardess continued brushing his lap.

"On a cow, it doesn't matter," Chiun snapped back, not turning away from the window.

"Hooray for common sense," Terri said.

"Fifth," Remo mumbled. "I'm sure it's fifth." He pressed his left index finger into the flight attendant's back. Her hands froze in position on his lap and a look of tranquillity came over her face.

Remo touched her cheek with his hand.

"Later," he said gently. Carefully, he turned her around and gave her a tiny push down the aisle toward the front of the plane.

As if she had no will of her own, she walked away, pausing to rest, leaning against a seat, then unsteadily lurching down the aisle.

"That was awful," Terri told Remo. She looked at the stewardess who was leaning against the bulkhead wall, her face wreathed in a smile. She seemed unable to move.

"What'd you do to her?" Terri asked.

"I just gave her something to remember me by. It was the only way to get her off me. You saw."

"How did you do it?"

"I don't know. I touched a nerve. You want one?" Remo asked.

"Keep your hands to yourself, you lecher."

"Just asking was all," Remo said.

Terri watched the stewardess. She had been leaning with her back against the wall, and slowly her feet slid out from under her. In a moment, she was sitting on the plane's floor.

"That's incredible," Terri said.

"It's a pain in the ass is what it is," Remo said. "Women sense it and they just won't leave me alone."

"I'll leave you alone. You know, you don't affect me at all. I don't even really like you."

"Oh?"

"That's right. Nothing. You do less than nothing for me. Zip code. My ideal man is cultured, noble, regal."

"And my ideal woman doesn't have a loose upper plate," Remo said.

Terri harrumphed, got up and stepped across Remo. She moved to the other side of the aisle and sat next to Chiun.

Chiun said, "I prefer to sit alone. Be gone, woman." He spun around and clamped his gaze on the wing again.

Terri rose and moved to a seat behind Remo.

He turned and smiled. "Welcome to the club. When he abuses you, he likes you."

"You must both love me then," she said.

"Only him," Remo said.

Smith regularly awoke at 5:29 A.M., one minute before his alarm was set to go off. Then he turned the clock off so that the ring would not disturb his wife.

By this day, he awoke at 5:24 A.M., a full five minutes early, and knew something was wrong. He must have been dreaming. But what was it about?

Then he remembered. It wasn't a dream. It had been a thought. The lunatic he had been talking to in the West somewhere had been talking about motion pictures.

Suddenly, it all made sense—his talking about gross points, his maundering about how everybody was stealing from him.

Somehow CURE's records had gotten into the information system of a moviemaker. No . . . a writer, as Smith recalled the conversation. Out there somewhere was a writer with CURE's records and now he was writing a screenplay based on the exploits of Remo and Chiun.

A small chill shuddered through Smith's body.

"Are you all right, dear?" his wife asked in the darkness of their bedroom in a little ranch house in Rye, New York.

"Yes. Why?"

"You're awake early," she said.

"Yes. I had an idea."

"How unusual," she said.

"Sorry to disturb you, dear," Smith said.

"Oh, you didn't disturb me."

"Go back to sleep, dear," Smith said.

"If you're sure everything's all right," she said.

"Everything's all right." Smith leaned over and pecked a kiss on his wife's cheek, then quickly left the bedroom to dress.

But Mrs. Smith knew something was wrong, two minutes later, when the alarm sounded. Smith had forgotten to turn it off, and that was something he hadn't done in twenty years.

Thirteen

His bags were flawless. The ammunition and auxiliary weapons were stashed neatly in lead-lined cavities on the inside of mock typewriters and dictating machines, so the airport's randomly used x-ray equipment would show only the familiar shape of those ordinary objects.

But most of Commander Hilton Marmaduke Spencer's arsenal was on his body, built into his suit, his shoes, his sleeves, his belts.

"How will you get past airport security?" Wissex had asked him.

"The same way I escaped from Moscow in 1964," Spencer had said. "Did I ever tell you? I was——"

"Well, I really have to go now," Wissex said. "Good luck on your mission."

"Luck has nothing to do with it, old top," Spencer said.

At London's Heathrow Airport, there was a long corridor leading to the waiting and boarding area for Air España planes. Only passengers were permitted past the human x-ray security machines that controlled the corridor.

Forty minutes before he was due to board, Spencer was at a cocktail lounge in the airport, waiting for someone to arrive.

"Stolichnaya, double," he ordered from the bartender.

"How do you like it, sir?" the bartender asked.

"Neat, of course," Spencer said. "And bring the pepper."

When the bartender came, he set the large shot glass in front of Spencer, along with the pepper shaker. Spencer sprinkled some of the spice on top of the liquor. The pepper grains floated there for a few moments, then slowly settled to the bottom of the glass.

Spencer looked up at the bartender and smiled. "The only way to drink vodka, don't you know," he said. "The pepper takes out the impurities and carries them to the bottom of the drink. What's left is pure vodka. I've always drunk it that way."

"I see it all the time," the bartender said in a bored voice. "I read about it once in a James Bond book. Even Yanks do it now."

"Until I told him about it," Spencer said frostily, "that man who wrote about James Bond used to drink his vodka with Coca Cola." His eyes defied the bartender to argue with him, but the man just drifted off toward another customer.

Spencer nursed his drink for about ten minutes until the man he had been waiting for showed up. The man was Spencer's size and wore an identical blue pinstripe suit with a red handkerchief in the lapel. Like Spencer, he had a rust-colored mustache and he wore an ecru-colored Panama straw hat. Standing alongside Spencer in the darkened bar, they looked like twins or an actor and his stunt double.

"Are you ready?" Spencer asked.

"As I'll ever be, Commander," the other man said.

"Synchronize watches," Spencer said. "Two forty-three and forty seconds. Forty-two. Forty-four."

"Got it," the other man said.

"All right," Spencer said. "At exactly 2:47, we move."

"Righto."

"Here's the ticket," Spencer said. He handed the other man his airline ticket and the man strolled off down the corridor toward the Air España loading gates.

Spencer drained the last of his vodka, careful not to disturb the pepper at the glass's bottom, which he knew was now contaminated with fuel oil. He thought about leaving the bartender a tip, but decided not to. Let his Yank friends who drank vodka and pepper leave him a tip. Spencer picked up his thin nylon gymnasium-style bag and stepped into the men's room next to the bar. Inside one of the toilet stalls, he took from the nylon bag a long doctor's robe, which he put on over his suit. A pair of dark wrap-around sunglasses covered his eyes. From the bottom of the nylon bag came a worn brown leather doctor's satchel.

Spencer rolled up the nylon gym bag and stuck it inside the waistband of his trousers. He checked his watch. Two forty-six and thirty-five seconds.

Almost time.

He stepped out of the men's room, just as the digital clicker of his watch registered the full minute.

Two forty-seven.

He heard a scream from down the Air España corridor. He ran toward the sound. Ahead of him, a group of people were clustered together.

"Let me through," Spencer called out in a heavy German accent. "I am a doctor. Let me through."

He ran past the x-ray detector machines and pushed his way through the crowd until he was next to the man with the red mustache. The man was lying on the floor, gasping for breath, his hands clutching his chest.

Professionally, Spencer knelt alongside the man and felt his pulse.

"Very serious," he said. "I vill need room to work. Stand back. All of you. *Schnell.*"

He hoisted the man into his arms and walked along the corridor toward the planes, then pushed his way through the door of the first men's room he reached.

It was vacant and the other mustached man quickly got to his feet. Spencer leaned against the door, keeping it closed, as he stripped off his doctor's robe. The other man put it on, along with Spencer's wrap-around sunglasses. He tucked Spencer's nylon gym bag into his waistband, turned, and glanced at himself in the mirror.

"Pretty neat if I do say so myself," he said. Spencer checked himself in the mirror on the back of the door. He heard people thumping outside.

"All right," he said. "Let's go. Ooops, the ticket." The man now wearing the doctor's costume handed Spencer the Air España ticket and then led the way through the door.

With the same thick German accent Spencer

had used, he said, "Everything isss all right. Lucky I vas here. Just a piece of candy stuck in ze throat. Lucky I vas here. I fixed him up all right."

Quickly, the man in the doctor's smock walked away. The eyes of the crowd followed him as Spencer stepped from the men's room and walked over to the Air España counter, where he got a boarding pass, then took a seat and buried his face in a magazine.

Three minutes later, the passengers were boarding, and five minutes later, his arms and legs wrapped with guns and rockets and knives and bombs, Commander Hilton Marmaduke Spencer was sprawled comfortably in a window seat in the plane's first-class cabin.

It had been a while, he thought, since he had an interesting assignment from Wissex. And these two, the Yank and the old Oriental, might be interesting. Eighteen men had already died trying to remove them. It might be fun.

Eighteen dead. It did not bother him. None of those eighteen had been Brits. Wait until the Yank and the Chink ran up against British steel.

He smiled, and the faint pounding began again inside his temples.

The union of motion pictures authors had been no help to Smith.

"I'm looking for a screenwriter," he had said, and the woman who had answered the phone had said, "Pick one. We've got seven thousand members."

"This one would probably have a word processor or computer," Smith said.

"That narrows it down to six thousand nine hundred," the woman said. "It's a great excuse not to work. They can't write movies but they sure as hell can play Pac-man. Got any more clues?"

"Maybe he's doing a script on Oriental assassins," Smith said hopefully.

"Not a chance," the woman said.

"Why not?"

"Nobody's doing assassins. Chopsaki. The movies never gross anything. Bruce Lee is dead but he was dead at the box office long before he died. Afraid I can't help you." And she hung up.

And that was it. Smith realized that he had no choice except to wait for the lunatic to call him again. The telephone rang.

"Smith here."

"You know who this is," the voice said.

"Yes," said Smith. "Except I don't have a name to put with the voice."

"That's all right. No matter what you call it, a rose is a rose."

"Obviously, you're the product of a classical education," Smith said.

"You know," said Barry Schweid, "I don't really trust you."

"I thought we were getting along fine," Smith said.

"We'll see when our negotiations go on," Schweid said.

"What negotiations? I gave you everything you asked for."

"That's why I don't trust you. What kind of producer are you anyway? I ask for 250 and you give me 250. What kind of crap is that? I ask for ten points and I get ten points. Gross points. Marlon Brando don't get points that easy and he wanted to play Superman's father in a suitcase."

Crazy, Smith thought. Hollywood had gotten to this one's brain, whoever he was. There was nothing left. What was he going to ask for now?

"Well, what is it you want?" Smith said.

"I've been giving it a lot of thought. I want three hundred fifty thousand and thirteen points."

Smith hesitated a moment. If he offered it, what would this madman want next? He thought for a split second, then reverted to his tight-fisted New England roots.

He slammed his fist on the desk.

"Not a chance," he shouted. "That's it. No three hundred fifty and no thirteen points. And no two hundred fifty or ten points either. The offer's now two hundred and eight points. Take it or leave it. You've got five seconds. One. Two——"

"Hold on; wait."

"No wait," Smith snarled. "I'm not going to be jerked around forever. Three. Four. Five——"

"Okay, okay," whined Barry Schweid. "You got a deal. Two hundred and eight points. I'll throw in a free rewrite. Don't tell the union."

"I don't know," Smith said. "It's a lot of money."

"One-ninety. I'll take one-ninety."

"Okay," Smith said after a pause. "now who the hell are you? You're not playing games with me anymore."

"All right. I'm Barry Schweid."

"Address and phone number. My lawyers will need it," Smith said.

Schweid rattled off the numbers and said, "I

don't know much about you, you know. Just who are you?"

"The person who's going to pay you one-ninety and eight points. I want that script in my hands the day after tomorrow." Smith gave him the number of a postal box in Manhattan. "Without fail. You got it?"

"Now you sound like a producer," said Schweid. "It'll be there."

"And I don't want a lot of copies floating around either," Smith said, and then hung up.

As he hung up the telephone, Smith smiled. Maybe he should start treating Remo that way. It might be more effective than trying to reason with him. It was a thought he decided to hold for a while.

And three thousand miles away, Barry Schweid replaced his telephone receiver. By trying to negotiate on his own, he had cost himself sixty thousand dollars and two points.

It wasn't fair. Producers were always taking advantage of writers. He decided he needed help, and the longer he thought, the more sure he was that he had exactly the right people to deal with one thieving producer.

Two thieving producers.

Bindle and Marmelstein.

Fourteen

The crowd sounded far away, but when they shouted "Olé," even the walls seemed to vibrate.

Remo groused, "This is getting absurd. Can't you take us anyplace without cows?" but Terri answered only with an annoyed "Shhhhh."

She was walking through a darkened tunnel, playing a flashlight on the walls. The only other illumination came from a single small lightbulb fixed to the stone ceiling of the tunnel thirty yards behind them and from a thin sliver of sunlight that snaked in under some kind of large wooden door twenty yards in front of them.

"Olé! Olé!" The crowd roared again.

"It's here somewhere," Terri said in exasperation, waving the flashlight angrily along the sweating stone walls. The air was musty, filled with sour dampness and the sweet decaying animal smell that reminded Remo of hamburgers. From back in the days when he was able to eat hamburgers.

Remo noticed that Chiun, standing alongside the woman, was rubbing the toe of his sandal in the white powder deposits on the stone floor, which years of dampness had washed from the tunnel's limestone walls. Chiun's toe scored the powder along the base of the walls, as if he were idly marking time, but Remo could tell, by the concentrated hunch of Chiun's shoulders, that he was not idling.

As Terry Pomfret continue to play her light on the walls, feeling the stone with her free hand, looking for something, anything, Chiun turned away to the other side of the tunnel and began to examine the powder on the floor there.

Toe pushed through the powder. Step. Toe again through the powder.

Remo was bored. He slumped down into a sitting position on the floor. The wall was cold and unyielding against his back and he felt its dampness through his thin black t-shirt. He watched Terri wandering around, shining her light, and Chiun wandering around, dragging his toe, and realized he was tired. Tired of the assignments, tired of the travel, tired of the same damn dullness of it all. He tried to think back to the days, so many years ago, before he had become one with Sinanju.

He had never thought of being an assassin then. He had been just a cop, his head filled with cop's ideas and cop's goals and cop's ambitions, most of which involved staying alive, not letting the bastards put a bullet in your belly, and getting out at age 55 after twenty years minimum service and spending the rest of his life fishing. He never even thought of assassins and didn't know that they existed.

But suppose he had thought about being an

assassin, what would he have thought? That it was an exciting glamorous life? The spies who came in from the cold? James Bond with exploding suitcases and poison pellets and a license to kill? One-man battles against the Mafia? Women sniffing around?

And what was the truth?

It was all of those things and none of them. It was Smith, always with a new assignment for him, always worrying about the end of the world, the end of civilization as we know it, the end of CURE. And Remo would grumble and take the assignment and almost all the assignments were wait, wait, wait. A few minutes of exercise and then more waiting. Only the exercise, the chance to use his skills, kept him happy and busy. The waiting just made him bored.

He watched Chiun push his toe through the dust.

Was Chiun bored too? Had thousands of years of Masters of Sinanju spent their lives in boredom and desperation, wishing something, anything, would happen?

No. It was the difference between Chiun and himself; the difference between the real Master of Sinanju and the young American who would someday be the next reigning Master of Sinanju.

Chiun could take each day as it came, each part of life as it happened, his being filled with an inner peace and kindness that came from knowing who and what he was. Remo was still unsure, confused, torn between the worlds of the West where he was born and the East where his spirit now lived. But Chiun was at rest with himself, and it made Remo envy his peaceful composure.

Chiun, still shuffling his feet through the limestone powder, had reached Remo. His sandaled foot touched Remo's.

"Move your feet, retard," Chiun said.

Remo looked down. His feet were in Chiun's way.

So much for inner peace, Remo thought. *Give me confusion every time.*

Chiun kicked him to make him move his feet.

Commander Spencer was among the first passengers to leave the plane in Madrid, but he had stopped short inside the boarding area when he saw another metal detector he would have to pass through.

He had no more mock doctors up his sleeve, but he allowed himself a smile when he thought of what he actually had up his sleeves: two heat-seeking portable missiles, designed for hand firing.

He turned back to the ramp to reboard the plane. The last passengers were leaving, giving the obligatory thanks to a male flight attendant of spurious goodwill and indeterminate sexual preference, whose primary contribution to the flight's bonhomie was to refuse anyone who asked a second bag of peanuts.

Spencer brushed by him.

"Left something on my seat," he said apologetically.

"Someone always does," the steward sniffed.

Spencer went toward the back of the plane, past his seat and into the small restroom where he locked the door, leaned against the sink, prepared himself and waited.

Five minutes later, the steward knocked on the door.

"Are you in there? You really shouldn't be in there. There are restrooms in the airport terminal. I must ask you to leave the plane now."

The restroom door opened and a strong arm reached out and yanked the steward inside.

With one smooth motion, Spencer cut his throat, then leaned the dying body over the sink, so that the blood from the wound would run into the sink and not down onto the steward's uniform.

Cramped in the close quarters, Spencer stripped the steward's uniform.

"Bloody look like bleeding pilots they do," he mumbled to himself. The uniform was not much of a fit, particularly over his blue pinstriped suit. But it would do.

He opened the door and peered out. The passenger cabin was empty. He shut the door behind him, ripped the lid from one of the passenger seat's ashtrays and jammed it as a wedge into the base of the door. It wouldn't keep anyone out, but it would hold long enough to convince somebody that a tool kit was needed to fix the recalcitrant door. By that time, Spencer would be gone.

A few moments later, he fell in with a group of blond stewardesses who had just gotten off a Pan-American plane. He listened to them chatter in some dogbark accent about the best places in Madrid to snare rich men. They all walked past the airport's metal detector and Spencer waved to the young woman on duty there. She smiled back at him and winked.

Boring, he thought. It was all so deadly boring. He hoped that the Yank and the Chink would at least be a moderate challenge, something to lift his flagging interest.

"Young woman, it is here," Chiun said.

Remo saw Chiun standing in front of a section of wall that looked to Remo no different from any other section. Terri, thirty feet away, hurried down to Chiun.

She shone the flashlight on the section of wall and said, "I don't see anyth . . . oh, there. Under the dirt."

"Yes," said Chiun.

With a handkerchief from her back pocket, Terri began to rub away at the gritty grime on the wall. Remo saw the first faint glimmering of gold begin to appear, reflecting dully in the beam of her flashlight.

Chiun backed away, toward Remo, to watch.

"How'd you know it was there?" Remo asked.

"The powder on the ground."

"Yeah? What about it?" Remo asked.

"You are really dense sometimes," said Chiun. "There was not as much of it there as elsewhere."

"What does that prove?"

"Is it not enough that I found the golden plaque? Must I be subjected always to this merciless cross-examination?" Chiun said.

"I just want to understand how you think," Remo said. "That's not merciless. Except to me."

"It is intrusive," Chiun said. "Everything is there for you to see. Why do you not see it?"

"Because I don't know what I'm supposed to see," Remo said.

"And if a man with his eyes screwed tightly closed asks what color the sky is and someone tells him, does that mean he can see the next sky with his eyes still closed?" asked Chiun.

"I don't know what the hell that means," said Remo.

"That is your problem, Remo. That is always your problem and it is why you will never amount to anything. You do not know what anything means."

"I'm not that bad. You're just ticked off because that Jap didn't have a Space Invaders game for you to play."

"Yes, you are that bad. But because it will be the only way I will ever have any peace on this earth, I will explain it to you. There is less of that lime powder on the wall here than there is anywhere else. What does that mean?"

"Probably that something disturbed it," Remo said. "Somehow removed the powder."

"Correct. Now since that is the only place in this godforsaken tunnel that is different, is it not reasonable to expect that there is a reason for its being different? A reason such as that plaque being on the wall?"

"I guess that's logical," Remo allowed.

"But that's not all," Chiun said.

"It never is," Remo said.

"Why would that plaque being there . . ." Chiun pointed to the wall where Terri Pomfret, oblivious to both of them, had finished scrubbing the encaked dirt from the golden plaque, ". . . Cause any change in the amount of powder there?" Chiun pointed to the floor at Terri's feet.

"Little Father?" Remo said.

"What?"

"Damned if I know," said Remo. "Or care."

"You are hopeless," Chiun said and walked away down the tunnel.

And because he didn't want Chiun to think he was hopeless, Remo tried to think, really think, about the significance of less powder on the floor. What could it mean? Had someone removed the powder? But why had they removed it in that spot? If they had, didn't it mean that someone knew the plaque was there?

He tried to think about it but his mind kept drifting away. Even in the semidarkness of the tunnel, he could see clearly because his eyes opened wide, like a cat's, to pull in every mote of available light. It was a matter of simple muscular control to one of Sinanju, a thing that even cheap cameras and binoculars were able to do, but that most people, whose eyes contained the most brilliantly devised lenses ever seen on earth, found impossible to imitate.

With his light-absorbing vision, he watched Terri Pomfret's rear end jiggle as she scrubbed away at the plaque and he soon forgot to think about the plaque and pleasantly thought about Terri's rear end.

He felt no guilt. It had often been his experience that when he tried to think about things, he could never think his way through them, but when he allowed himself to forget them, then the answer to the problem often jumped into his mind of its own accord. As if it were just waiting there, ready to solve itself, but it just wouldn't do it until he stopped bothering it.

Maybe that would happen now and he would impress Chiun. But it wouldn't happen if he kept staring at Terri Pomfret's rear end, clad tightly in faded blue denims whose softness seemed only to hint at the softness under them, whose velvet texture he could almost feel under his fingers, whose. . . .

He concentrated on the limestone powder on the floor. He saw Chiun coming back down the tunnel toward them. And he heard Terri say, "Oooohhhh." It was a long, sad, disappointed sound and when she turned to face Remo, her face was sitting Shiva.

"What's the matter?" he said.

"It isn't here," she said.

"What's new?" Remo said. "It hasn't been anywhere we've gone."

"This is new," Terri said. "It's not here and it's not anywhere."

Bullfights were really rather dull. Oh, perhaps they were all right for Spanish heathen who liked to see miniature men in tights and ballet shoes dancing around in front of a dumb beast, but somehow it left Spencer's blood unmoved.

"Olé, indeed," he muttered to himself. The crowd hushed as the matador drew the short curved sword from under the muleta. Slowly, holding the small cape at waist height and peering down the length of the sword which he held near his shoulder, the torero advanced on the poor confused bull, which stood in the middle of the arena, bleeding, sweating, tormented. If the beast had had a brain to wonder with, he would be wondering why he was being taunted by this young jackrabbit, Spencer thought, even as the bull, with the bravery born of stupidity, charged the red cape one more time and the matador plunged the curved blade down behind the bull's neck, and rolled off to the left to escape the bull's right horn. The blade curved down, severing the spinal cord and piercing a lung before cutting into the beast's giant heart.

The bull stopped leadenly in its tracks, and then, like a newsreel film of an exploded building collapsing, seemed to come apart in sections. First it dropped to its knees and then its rear legs collapsed and then it coughed, a hacking spray of blood that spotted the sand for fifteen feet in front of his body, and then it pitched onto its side and quietly, heroically, stupidly died.

The crowd leaped to its feet cheering for the torero who now strutted around the ring, looking up at the spectators, waving his hat to the ladies, curiously mincing in his walk, as the fans shouted their approval of his bravery in the face of death.

And Commander Hilton Marmaduke Spencer, O.G., K.L.M., D.S.C., thought it was all kind of disgusting and pointless, fit only for the brutish unwashed, and got up from his chair and started downstairs to kill people.

Terri looked away from Remo to Chiun. "It says there's no gold," she said. She turned back toward the plaque and illuminated it with the flash-light in her hand. "It says——"

Chiun spoke softly. "It says 'Look no further. The gold is no more. You will not find it.' "

Terri wheeled around. "How did you know?"

"It was many years ago," Chiun said, "in the time of the Master Hup To. He came to Hamidia to do something for the chief of the golden people there. That master learned the language of the people and masters pass these things along." He looked at Remo. "Except some masters who are so unfortunate as to have no one to pass wisdom along to. The life of some is spent in having to shout into cracks in mountains, wishing they were ears."

"I've got it," Remo yelled.

"Keep it," Chiun said.

Terri asked Chiun, "Why didn't you tell me you read ancient Hamidian?"

"Because it was not necessary. You have translated all correctly and have missed nothing. Until now," Chiun said.

"No, I've really got it," Remo yelled again. He got to his feet.

"Be quiet," Terri said. She asked Chiun, "What have I missed?"

Do you not notice something strange about the carvings that made these letters?" Chiun asked.

"No," Terri answered slowly. "They're all the same. Wait."

"That's it," Remo said. "they're all the same." He talked fast so no one would interrupt. "They're all the same because they were all written by the same person. That's why there's less powder on the ground under the plaque. Because somebody disturbed it when he came here to hang the plaque. That's why. It was probably the same guy who hung the plaques all over. That's how it was. I figured it out. Me." He looked at Chiun, who ignored him and looked at Terri. Then Remo looked at Terri, who ignored him to look at Chiun.

Terri said, "The writing's exactly the same. That shouldn't be. There should be differences if the plaques were engraved by different people at different times. They were all written by just one person."

"Exactly," Chiun said.

"You knew," Terri said.

"Only when I felt the edges of the writing here," Chiun said. "Along the straight lines of the engraving, there is a nick. It comes from a flaw in the chisel used to cut it. There was the same flaw in the other plaques. Written by the same man, with the same tool, at the same time."

"I figured it out," Remo said. "I figured it out."

"Who cares?" Terri snapped at him. "Probably done in one place at one time," she told Chiun.

"Correct," the old man said. "No one could have traveled that far to engrave plaques all over the world. Not in ancient days. The Hamidian boats were just too slow. They were made for cargo, and there is a saying in Sinanju that when offered a Hamidian voyage, one is better off swimming because it is faster."

"I knew it," Remo said. "I knew it." He touched Chiun's shoulder. "It was the powder on the ground," he said. "Somebody moved it when he was hanging this plaque."

Chiun continued to look at Terri, whose face was illuminated in the glow of the flashlight she held at her waist.

"But why?" Terri asked. "Why would somebody go to all the trouble and expense of forging these plaques for us to find?"

"Because someone wants us to do just what we have been doing," Chiun said. "There is another thing also. There have always been stories of mountains of gold. But there has never been found a mountain of gold."

Terri shook her head. "Who wants us to do what we are doing? I don't understand."

They were interrupted by the sound of a trumpet, playing the Spanish march of the invitation to the bull.

Then behind them, they heard another sound. There was the noise of heavy hooves and the ugly snorting sound of an enraged bull; and then the beast, a whole half-ton of him, stomped around the far corner of the tunnel. He stopped under the bare light bulb. His eyes, fixed on the three humans, were narrowed and malevolent. Heavy breath came from his nostrils, its hot moisture creating little puffs of fog in the damp tunnel. His tail swished back and forth.

"Oh, crap," Terri said.

"Big Mac is here," said Remo.

Several women smiled warmly at Commander Spencer as he walked down the bleacher steps of the Plaza de Toros. He brushed against one woman and murmured an apology.

"Señor, you can bump me anytime," she said, her doe-eyes flashing at him.

"Perhaps later," Spencer said, without breaking stride. His mind was not on women. His mind was on the game. The quarry waited and he was the hunter.

The tiny pulses in his temple were beginning to throb again.

The bull stood his ground. Remo, Chiun, and Terri looked at the big animal, then suddenly, the tunnel behind them was bathed in bright light. Remo glanced over his shoulder. The giant doors behind them leading to the sunlit arena had been opened, and standing in the center of the sand-floored arena, framed in the rectangle of the doorway as if it were a camera viewfinder, were a matador and two picadors on horseback.

Remo looked back at the bull and Chiun said, "Remo, please dispose of that thing."

"You never showed me how to do bulls."

"You can't see things. You can't do bulls. What good are you?" Chiun asked.

"I'm good in bed," Remo said.

"Will you two stop bickering and do something about that beast?" Terri said.

Remo stepped forward in the tunnel and called out, "Heyyyy, toro." He turned to Terri. "How do you like that? I saw it once in an Anthony Quinn movie."

Terri turned toward the sunlit entrance to the tunnel. "I'm getting out of here," she said, but Chiun reached out, took her arm and stopped her.

"We do not know what is out there. Someone

brought us here. Someone may wait out there for you."

"Damned if I do and damned if I don't," Terri said, just as the bull charged.

Spencer was in the front row of seats, just behind the high wooden fence. He put a hand atop the thick wooden boards and lightly vaulted over the rail, dropping the eight feet into the sand of the arena below.

The crowd saw him and let out a surprised hiss, then began chattering nervously to themselves as Spencer marched across the sand toward the open doors of the tunnel.

The matador ran up to stop him, but without breaking stride the Englishman backhanded him across the face and he dropped into the sand as if felled with an axe. Then the Englishman in the dark-blue suit reached the tunnel entrance and stepped inside.

Remo was showing off. The bull had pulled up in its charge and Remo had dropped down on his knees so that his nose touched that of the giant creature.

From the side of his mouth, Remo said to Terri, "Wheeew, some breath. How do you like this?"

But Terri did not answer. Another voice did, a man's voice. Spencer stood in the archway, and said with a voice surprisingly devoid of malice, "Not bad, Yank. Too bad you won't have time to pursue it as a career."

With one smooth motion, Spencer slipped off

his jacket and dropped it onto the floor of the tunnel, then pulled the doors shut behind him.

Strapped to each shirt-sleeve was a thin, eight-inch-long bomb that looked like a fireworks rocket. Spencer peeled one from the snap holder around his left forearm, then laid it over his arm and aimed it down the tunnel toward Remo. He twisted a small pin at the back of the missile and with a whooshing hiss, it flamed off down the tunnel.

Remo rose and turned, but he had no time to raise his arms or react to the weapon. Before it struck him, Chiun flashed across in front of Remo, his yellow robe a blurring fuzzy sun in the semilit tunnel. The side of his hand touched the rocket and it soared over Remo's shoulder to explode against the rear wall of the tunnel.

Without looking, Remo reached behind him and rapped the bull between the eyes with the side of his hand.

"Go to sleep, Ferdinand," he said. The bull moaned and fell onto its side, unconscious. Remo took a step toward the Englishman in the doorway, but Spencer had already ripped the second missile loose from his right forearm. Chiun grabbed Terri and ran down the tunnel and Remo followed.

Behind him, he heard the high-pitched sound of Spencer's vicious laughter.

Chiun hissed, "I know these boom-shooters. They seek out the heat of the human body."

They passed under the small light bulb that illuminated the far end of the tunnel. A thick iron door blocked their way out of the maze which wandered under the arena's stands. When they turned, their backs to the stone wall, Spencer was moving toward them. He stepped over the unconscious downed bull.

"Just step toward me, Missie," Spencer said to Terri. "I don't want to have to hurt you, you know."

Terri said, nodding dumbly, "I understand."

Remo said, "You understand? He's trying to kill us and you understand? Lady, put your oars in the water."

Remo looked toward Chiun. He knew the two of them could take off through the iron door and escape but Terri would be too slow, too vulnerable. Their fleeing would cost her her life.

Chiun was staring straight ahead at the burly Englishman but the stare was one of neither threat nor fear. It was a curious, dead stare as if Chiun were embalmed, the look of a man dead, but with his eyes wide open and staring. The color had drained from Chiun's face and in the flickering overhead light; he looked ghostlike.

He stepped forward to meet Spencer.

The Englishman had stopped twenty feet from them. Behind him, Remo heard the sound of the trumpet blaring again from the bull arena.

Now Chiun was only three feet from Spencer.

"Out of the way, old man," Spencer said.

Chiun shook his head, sadly and with finality. Remo noticed how stiffly Chiun moved, as if the life already had gone from him. What was he doing?

"Have it your own way, sir," Spencer said.

From only three feet away, he aimed the missile at the center of Chiun's forehead. Then he twisted the firing mechanism on the back of the rocket. It shot forward with a hiss, but then, seemingly by magic, it veered upward and exploded against the overhead lightbulb.

Terri inhaled her breath noisily as Chiun slowly extended a finger toward Spencer and touched the Briton's cheek.

"It's cold," Spencer said. "You're cold."

Remo nodded. Of course. The only defense against bombs that sought out the heat of a human body was an inhumanly cold body.

"Cold," Spencer said again.

"As you soon will be," Chiun said slowly. "Remo, remove this one."

"You're there," Remo said. "You do it."

"You need the practice," Chiun said.

Remo sighed and released Terri's arm.

"All right, I'll do it. But I'm getting tired of being the schlepp around here. Wait. We ought to question him. Find out what's going on with these phony inscriptions. Good idea, Chiun. I'll do it."

"I don't think either of you will be doing anything quite so easily," Spencer said. "You ever see one of these before?" He pulled a small black ball that looked like a regulation handball from a clip on the back of his belt.

"Naaah," Remo said. "Chiun, you ever see one of those before?"

"No," Chiun said. "Ask him if it plays Space Invaders."

"I don't think it does," Remo said. He moved past Chiun as the old man went back to guard Terri.

"It's a deadly fragmentation bomb," Spencer said. "Blow you to bits, Yank."

"Naaah," Remo said. "That stuff never works. It never goes off and if it does go off, it busts up windows and nothing else."

He heard Chiun behind him. "The British always used toys. That is why they never amounted to anything."

"I know, Little Father," Remo said.

Spencer's face reddened in anger. "We will see," he said. Softly, underhanded, he tossed the fragmentation bomb at Remo, then ran back toward the entrance to the tunnel. Remo picked up the bomb and held it in his hand. He could feel it whirring. There was an explosive charge inside of it, and when it went, it would break through the metal covering, which was already scored to break apart in jagged-edged pieces. But just as water could not rush into an already-full vessel, an explosive force could not explode against a containing force that was exactly its equal.

It would be stalemate: an irresistible force pushing an immovable object, neither giving way until the power of the force just passed its vibrations off into the stillness of the surrounding air. Remo felt the bomb still whirring inside his hand. He stretched his fingers to see if his hand could contain the entire sphere, but it was slightly too large. Some parts of the metal remained uncovered and the explosive force would break through there, and then the whole bomb would blow apart, taking Remo's hand with it.

He cupped his left hand over his right. The delicate flesh of his hands felt the coldness of the metal held inside. He softened his hands, relaxing his muscles, until he was sure that the entire surface of the spherical bomb was touched by his flesh. Then he began to exert pressure. That was the tricky part—to have the pressure forcing inward exactly equal to the pressure blasting outward at the moment of explosion.

He felt a click as the bomb's firing mechanism went off. Inside his hands, he felt the sudden buildup of pressure against his left ring finger and his right pinky. Instinctively, he increased downward pressure of those two fingers. His hands held and the explosion stayed muffled in his hands.

He could feel the pressure waves of the dissipating force vibrate the air around his hands and then the waves reached his face. He could see them shimmer against the light from the partially open doorway at the end of the tunnel. For a split second his arms twitched in the eddy of the force currents. Then the blast slowed down and in another second, the force had leaked harmlessly into the air.

Remo opened his hands and looked at the pure, unbroken black sphere. He tossed it toward Spencer. "Told you. You can't trust these things."

Spencer recoiled as the bomb hit the stone floor in front of him and rolled harmlessly away.

The Englishman reached down to the back of his shoe, snapped a pellet from the back of his heel, and tossed it onto the ground in front of Remo. It popped, almost a firecracker's pop, and a dark billow of smoke rose, surrounding Remo's face. He stopped breathing, in case it was poison. Spencer pulled a throwing knife from the back of his belt, raised it over his head, and propelled it at the center of the smoky mist, at the spot where Remo's chest would be.

An ordinary man would have been defenseless, unable to see to protect himself against the razor-sharp blade flying toward him. But mist and smoke, Remo knew, were not just one thing; they were a bundle of bits, just as television was not one picture, continuously moving, but a series of still pictures flashed at the rate of thirty per second. It took the cooperation of the average person's mind and eyes to make them into a moving picture.

So with smoke. It did not have to blind or obscure if a person simply realized that it was made up of separate particles. Then he could focus on the particules with primary vision, changing the fog and smoke to a transparent drizzle, and then use secondary vision to see the object behind the smoke.

This Remo did and saw the knife flying toward his chest.

Spencer saw the knife disappear into the column of smoke that was Remo. He expected the usual thud and scream when it bit flesh, but there was no thud and no scream.

Instead there was silence. Then a snap, a hard, metallic cracking sound. And then two halves of the knife, the handle and the blade, came flying back from the mist to land on the stone floor at Spencer's feet.

"Oh, bloody, shit," said Spencer.

Wissex had warned him that these two were dangerous but had not prepared him for this. It was time for Old Reliable. As the smoke dissipated and Remo's form again became visible, Spencer reached into a shoulder holster and withdrew a Pendleton-Sellers .31 caliber semimag automatic with the Bolan augmented armature. The pistol fired a shell that exploded into fragments a foot away from the muzzle of the gun. Anything in the immediate area would be downed. It could level a cocktail party of people faster than Norman Mailer talking prison reform could level common sense.

Spencer pulled the slide back to put a shell into the firing chamber. As he did, he backed away from Remo, lest the crazy American make a suicidal lunge.

"Don't back up any more," Remo said.

"An old trick, Yank."

"I'm warning you. Don't go any further."

"You're the one who's going, pally," said Spencer.

Too late, Spencer heard the roar. He wheeled just as the bull rammed into him. The beast's large, curved horns dug deep into the Englishman's belly and the bull lifted him, impaled on the horns, up over his head. The bull stopped and looked at Remo as if he recognized him, then turned and crashed away down the tunnel toward the partially open doors.

The trumpet player was in full throat but his music died in a squawk as the bull broke out into the sunshine, his cargo of dead Englishman avast on his horns.

The crowd screamed.

Remo walked back to Terri and Chiun.

"Damn," he said. "I wanted to get some answers from him."

"He was very brave," Terri said.

"Your dream man, huh? Good. The next one to come after us, I'll let him have you," Remo said.

"You didn't have anything to do with it," Terri said. "His bomb didn't go off. And his knife fell apart before it hit you. And the bull got him before he could shoot you."

"Lady," Remo said.

"What?"

"You're an asshole." Remo turned his back on her and said to Chiun, "I wish I knew who sent him."

"I know who sent him," Chiun said.

"You do? Who? How?"

"Did you not see the crest on his jacket?"

"No."

"Then you did not see the crest on the jackets of the others who tried to kill us?" Chiun said.

"No."

"The same crest will be on that knife," Chiun said.

Remo trotted back down the tunnel and picked up the hilt of the knife. He looked at it as he walked back to Chiun. A lion, a sheaf of wheat, and a dagger.

"What is it?" Remo asked.

"The House of Wissex," Chiun said.

"Who the hell are they?"

"Some upstart Englishmen," Chiun said. "I thought we had taught them a lesson." He shook his head sadly. "But some people never learn."

Fifteen

"Here's a big one." Hank Bindle was looking at the pictures in *Variety's* International Film Annual and he stopped to point out a full-page ad to Bruce Marmelstein.

"What's it about?" Marmelstein asked, craning his neck to look at the page.

"I don't know," Bindle said. "Let's see. It's got a picture of an airplane and a girl falling off a building and a guy with a sword."

"New guy or old guy?" asked Marmelstein.

"Old guy, you know, wearing like some kind of fur. With muscles. Like Conan. And there's like a missile heading for the city."

"Sounds like Conan meets Superman. I didn't hear that anybody's doing that," Marmelstein said. "You can't read any of the words?"

"I think this one is *the*. Is *the* T-H-E?"

"I think that's *the*. He pronounced it thee.

"What's the difference between *the* and *thee?*" Bindle drew out the long sound of the syllable.

"They're different words," Marmelstein said. "That much I know."

"What about when you say *the* book and *thee* apple?" Hank Bindle said, scratching his head in bewilderment. "You mean they're different words?"

"Well, how could they be the same word if you sound one *the* and the other one *thee?*" Marmelstein asked. He twisted the chains around his neck as he always did when he was involved in a deep philosophical discussion.

"You just did it," Bindle said.

"Did what?"

"You said *the* same word and then you said *thee* other one. You used both of those words in the same sentence."

Marmelstein smiled warmly. "I sure did, didn't I?"

"You know a lot of words, Bruce," said Bindle.

"You have to work hard to stay ahead of the crowd. It's a jungle out there."

"You know," Bindle said, "I'm glad we both know now that the other one can't read. It's made us closer, kind of."

"Partners should always be honest," Marmelstein said.

"Right," said Bindle.

"Good. Now who can we rip off?" Marmelstein asked. "Did the new incorporation come in?" asked Bindle.

"Yes," said Marmelstein. "Just today. So now we have a new corporate structure."

"I hope we keep this one longer than a week," Bindle said. "I always have trouble remembering the names of whatever corporation we're supposed to be each week."

"Just leave the business side of it to me," Marmelstein said. "You know, I wish I knew what that Barry Schweid was up to."

"Yeah," said Bindle. "He's got some nerve going to another producer."

"Especially after we produced his other movies. *Teeth. Space Battle. Distant Encounters of the First Kind.*"

"Don't forget *On Silver Lake,*" Bindle said.

"That's right. We've done some good ones." Marmelstein said. "A few more and we might even think about stopping selling cocaine."

"I don't know about that," said Bindle. "There's a lot of money in cocaine."

"Are we interested in money or creating enduring cinematic art?" Marmelstein asked. He pronounced it "cinemackic."

The two partners looked at each other for a few long seconds as the question hung in the air, unanswered. Finally, they nodded.

"Right. Money," they said in unison.

The telephone rang inside Marmelstein's desk. The desk was a large pink Italian marble slab, resting at both ends on two slices of highly-varnished wood cut from redwood trees. On Marmelstein's side of the desk, the redwood had been hollowed out so that a file cabinet could fit into each side of the pedestal.

There was nothing in the file cabinet except the telephone. Marmelstein thought it was tacky to have a telephone on the desk. He had gotten that idea when he first came to Hollywood and went into a producer's office and there was no telephone on the desk. It was the only real producer's office he had ever been in and he assumed that all producers spurned the telephone, especially since he had never been able to reach any of them by phone. If he had been able to read, he would have seen in the local press the week after he had met the phoneless producer that the producer had been indicted for embezzlement, for diverting money to his own personal use and letting production company bills go unpaid. Among the unpaid bills was the telephone bill. His phone had been removed by Earth Mother Bell, the Hollywood phone company.

Marmelstein opened the desk drawer, but before he answered the phone, he said to Bindle, "Listen to the new name."

He lifted the receiver.

"Hello. Universal Bindle Marmelstein Mammoth Global Magnificent Productions speaking. How may we help you?"

He smiled at Bindle. The name of the company had been carefully chosen to allow the two partners to tell people that they were with Universal and mumble the rest of the words, or that they were with MGM, short for Mammoth Global Magnificent. Every little bit helped, Marmelstein thought. And often said.

"Bruce, this is Barry Schweid. I want you to help me."

"That's what I said on the phone. 'How may we help you?' " Marmelstein said. "Right after I said Universal Bindle Marmelstein Mammoth Global Magnificent Productions. That's our new name."

"Yeah, yeah, I know all that. I want you to come in as partners on one of my movies. Minor partners," Schweid said.

"We'll start raising money immediately," Marmelstein said. "Do story boards. Talk to directors and stars. There's still time for us to——"

"No," Schweid said. "You're going to get an agent's cut. That's all. I already got a producer."

"What do you want us to do?"

"Negotiate for me," Schweid said. "I think this guy is screwing me."

"What do you want that he won't give?" asked Marmelstein.

"That's just it. He's giving me everything I want."

"I don't trust him," Marmelstein said.

"When I asked him for money, he said yes," Schweid said.

"He's a thief," Marmelstein said.

"I wanted gross points, he gave me gross points."

"Oh, the dirty bastard. Trying to work you over that way," Marmelstein said. "It's hard for me to believe sometimes what kind of thieves there are in this town."

"I need you two," Schweid said. "I know you're drug peddlers but you know how to negotiate."

"You've come to the right place, Barry. Just tell me what you want."

"All I want is what I got. But I don't want him to be so damn agreeable about it," Schweid said.

"We'll end that," Marmelstein promised. "When do we see this guy?"

"I'll talk to him tonight on the phone. A conference call. You guys can take over," Schweid said.

"You've got it. We'll straighten him out."

After Marmelstein hung up, he rubbed his hands together and looked at Hank Binde.

"We're back in with Schweid," he said. "He's got a producer for a movie but he doesn't trust him."

"He can trust us," Bindle said.

"That's what I told him."

"What movie?" Bindle asked.

"I don't know. He said art. Probably that *Hamlock* thing."

"I think it's *Hamlet*," Bindle said.

"Yeah. *Hammerlet*. With tits. I hope this guy wants to do it with tits."

"What's in it for us?" Bindle asked.

Marmelstein started to answer, then paused. "Wait," he said. "Listen, anybody can do *Hammerlet*, right? I mean, the screenwriter died or something and so it belongs to everybody?"

"Yeah. I think it was a play. Shakespeare. Or some name like that."

"Okay," Marmelstein said. "What we do is we get this producer away from Schweid. If that no-talent can write *Hammerlock*, we get can somebody else to write *Hammerlock* and then we take it back to that same producer. Without Schweid."

"Good thinking, Bruce," said Bindle.

"All we've got to do is queer this deal tonight," Marmelstein said.

"Right," said Bindle.

"And that shouldn't be any trouble for us at all," Marmelstein said.

"It never has been before," said Hank Bindle.

* * *

Chiun was on the balcony of their Madrid hotel room, sitting quietly, looking at the city sprawl, the buildings golden in the afternoon sun.

Remo placed a call to Smith. The operator did a lot of clicking and then reported in precise English, "I'm sorry, sir. The line is busy."

"Are you sure?" Remo said. "That line's never busy. Maybe we dialed wrong." He repeated the number.

"Just a moment," the woman said. Remo heard more clicking, and then a busy signal and then the operator's voice. "No, sir, it's busy."

"Thank you," Remo said. "I'll call back."

He hung up the phone and stood up from the sofa. Somehow a busy signal didn't seem right. In all the years with CURE, he couldn't remember Smith not answering the phone on the first ring.

A busy signal made the CURE director seem more human and Remo didn't want to deal with Smith as a human. He didn't necessarily like the bloodless, emotionless wraith he pictured in his mind, but at least he was used to Smith that way. Every time things had changed in his life, they had changed for . . . well, if not for the worse, at least in the direction of more disruption. He didn't want any more disruption, irritation, or aggravation.

Peace and quiet. That was what he yearned for.

"That's what I want in the world," he said as he stepped out on the balcony behind Chiun.

"A brain that works?" Chiun said.

"Please, Chiun. Don't carp. I've made a resolution to myself. From now on, I'm going to lead a simple life, clean and pure. No more trouble. I'm going to try not to fall asleep when you recite an Ung poem. When you blame it all on me because you can't finish your screenplay or your soap opera about Sinanju, I'm just going to nod and take the blame. I'm going to lead a different life. When that dingaling Dr. Pomfret starts yapping at me, I'm just going to smile. When I talk to Smith, I'm going to humor him instead of arguing. Even when you tell me those stupid stories you always tell me, I'm going to listen. Really listen."

"By stupid stories, I presume you mean the wisdom of the ages, contained in the legends of Sinanju," Chiun said, without turning.

"That's right."

"The dog can promise not to bark," Chiun said, "but still he barks. Even the promise is expressed in a bark."

"Yeah?" Remo said. "Go ahead. Tell me a story. Watch me listen. Tell me about the mountain of gold. What's that about? I know you know more about it than you've been telling that twit."

"It is a terrible story. I don't want to talk about it," Chiun said.

"Awwww, please," said Remo, because he knew Chiun wanted him to.

"Really?" said Chiun. "You insist on hearing it?"

"My life wouldn't be complete without it," Remo said. "I'd go to my grave wondering what it was."

"Well, all right," Chiun said. "But only because you asked. It is a terrible story."

"The deal's off. If you do anything, we'll sue you for every cent you can borrow."

"Wait a minute," Harold W. Smith said. "Who is this?"

"This is Bruce Marmelstein, executive vice-president and chief financial officer of Universal Bindle Marmelstein Mammoth Global Magnificent Productions and we're prepared to top any paltry, piddling illegal offer you think you may have made to Barry Schweid."

Schweid's voice piped in. "That's right, Smith. Any offer."

"So now it's up to you, Smith," said Marmelstein. "Make an offer."

"What do you want, Schweid?" Smith asked.

"A half a million dollars and twenty percentage points. Gross," said Schweid.

"You've got it," Smith said.

"There you go again," said Schweid. "See. He's doing it again."

"We'll top it," Marmelstein yelled.

"That's right," shouted Hank Bindle. "We know a winner when somebody reads it to us."

"I'll give you six hundred thousand and twenty-two points," Smith said.

Before Schweid could answer, Marmelstein yelled, "Chickenfeed. We'll top it. You're not going to screw our friend Barry with these pittances of offers."

"That's right," said Hank Bindle. "No pitnesses of offers."

Smith said, "Barry, listen to me and think for a moment. Six hundred thousand dollars. And twenty-two points of the gross. And I'll have the six hundred thousand dollars in your hands in forty-eight hours. In a certified check. All yours. That's cash. Not a promise. You want to turn that down?"

Marmelstein shouted, "Are you inferring that our word is no good? That our credit's bad?"

"Yeah. Don't you ever infer that," warned Bindle.

"Well," said Barry Schweid. His voice was hesitant.

"You're not conning him like that, Smith," said Marmelstein. "You think you're talking to some greenhorn? Barry Schweid is one of the most brilliant writers in Hollywood. What he did for us on *Teeth* and *On Silver Lake* was absolute genius. What's six hundred thousand dollars to him?"

"Wait a minute," Barry told Marmelstein. "Six hundred thousand is a lot of money."

"A pitness," Bindle said.

"We'll top it," Marmelstein said. "Goodbye, Smith. We've got nothing more to talk about. You've insulted Barry so much he can never work with you."

Smith heard the phone click off in his ear. So that was that. He thought the whole thing had been a simple mistake and he would be able to buy CURE's records back from Barry Schweid. But now, with these other two in it, things had changed. Schweid was no longer just an annoyance, he was a menace. The three of them had become Remo Williams' next assignment.

Remo.

Where was Remo?

Why hadn't he called?

The telephone rang again and Smith answered.

"Smith, this is Bruce Marmelstein."

"I thought we were done talking," Smith said.

"No, that was just for Schweid's benefit. He's a schmuck. You really want this movie?"

"Yes."

"Six hundred thousand dollars worth?" asked Marmelstein.

"Yes, I'll pay that."

"We'll save you a hundred thou. You've got a deal at 500,000 dollars. But it goes to us. That's Universal Bindle Marmelstein Mammoth Global Magnificent Productions."

"You don't own it. It's Schweid's property," Smith said.

"That doesn't matter. Tonight we'll tell him our deal fell through. We lost our backers. We'll get him to sell it to us cheap and tomorrow we'll give it to you."

"That's wonderful," Smith said.

"Good," said Marmelstein. "We're going to do the best *Hammerlet* you ever saw."

"*Hamlet?*" asked Smith.

"Right. The immortal Barf of Afton. *Hammerlet*. Am I saying it right?"

"You're saying it fine," Smith said.

"Who needs Schweid to write *Hammerlet?* Everybody can write *Hammerlet*," said Marmelstein. "You'll have a movie to be proud of. 'Mr. Smith presents *Hammerlock*, a Universal Bindle Marmelstein Mammoth Global Magnificent Production.' You'll love it."

"I can't wait," Smith said.

"You'll hear from us," Bruce Marmelstein said.

"And you'll hear from me," Smith said as he replaced the phone in the darkened office.

"It happened just a few years ago," Chiun said. "About the time that Columbus was stumbling all over your country."

"Chiun, that was 500 years ago."

"Yes. So it was not long ago and there was a master then and his name was Puk. You may not believe this, Remo, but sometimes the Masters of Sinanju have not been nice. And sometimes they have not been flawless. Some have not been perfect human beings, even though you find that hard to believe."

"I'm absolutely devastated by the news," Remo said.

"As well you might be, it being so alien to your experience," Chiun said. "At any rate, this master, whose name was Puk, left the village of Sinanju one day without explanation. He told none of the villagers where he was going and none could guess.

"He was gone three years. Three years without report and without sustenance to the village and many babies were sent home to the sea then. In the old days, Remo, when we could not feed our babies, we——"

"I know, Chiun," said Remo. "You drowned them and called it sending them home to the sea. I've heard it hundreds of times."

"Please don't interrupt," Chiun said. "Then one day, Puk returned to our village. He was filled with wondrous tales of the faraway land he had visited. It was in a place no one had ever heard of, in what you now call South America, and he told of the wonderful battles he had fought and how he had brought honor to Sinanju. And most of all, he told of how the country he had visited had a mountain of gold.

" 'So where is this bounty?' the villagers cried, and Puk said 'It is coming.' But it did not come and Puk found himself an outcast in his village with none believing him."

Remo said, "South America. That's where Hamidia is. He went to Hamidia."

"Yes," said Chiun. "But he brought back no mountain of gold. Everyone talks about mountains of gold, but no one has ever seen one, it seems. No one except Puk, that is, and who could believe Puk?"

"Is that how you learned to speak Hamidian?" Remo asked.

"That was another master some time later. He went to Hamidia, but he never mentioned any mountain of gold."

"So it's a fairy tale," Remo said.

"For all we know," said Chiun.

"Okay. What happened to Puk?"

"Puk had many assignments around Korea for the rest of his life and helped support the village but he was never truly forgiven for the terrible story he told about the mountain of gold. And when he died, there were none of the ceremonies that usually attend the death of a master. In fact, few mourned. The villagers wrote a song instead. It said, 'Puk, those who would have mourned were sent to the sea while you were out chasing moonbeams. If you seek mourners, go to the bottom of the sea.' "

"It's a sad story," Remo said.

"Yes," said Chiun. "Puk did work in Hamidia and didn't get paid for it. That is very sad. Anyway, when you come next to Sinanju, I will show you Puk's grave. The headstone says, 'Here lies Puk the liar. Still lying.' "

Remo left Chiun on the balcony, still shaking his head over the irresponsible liar, Puk. This time the operator got his call through quickly and Smith answered it on first ring.

Quickly, Remo filled him in on what had happened and said, "A scam, Smitty. That's all it was. I don't know why but somebody faked all those plaques and put them around. Chiun says it has something to do with some British assassins, the House of Unisex or something. Yeah, the girl's all right. I think she's mad at me for getting rid of the last Limey who tried to kill her. I don't know. She's wacky. Something about him being her dream man. Anyway, that's the bottom line. No mountain of gold. The dip is out shopping. Naturally. We'll be leaving here tomorrow. No, she doesn't know who we are."

Remo paused and listened as Smith rapid-fired instructions into the phone.

"Hold on," Remo said. "I've been halfway around the world and I need a rest. I don't want to go to Hollywood. Sure, it's important, everything's always important. No, no, no. We; We'll talk about it when I get back. Smitty, you're babbling. *Ham-*

let and assassin movies and producers and points. Take a Valium. We'll talk when I get back. All right, all right, if you want them gone, they'll be gone. That make you feel better?" He listened to Smith's answer, then slammed down the phone.

"Yeah, sure," he grumbled to himself. "Thanks for telling me it was a good job. Sure. In a pig's ass. I'm tired of being unappreciated."

Sixteen

"*Cuanto?*" asked Terri Pomfret.

"For you, Madam, six dollars."

"*Es demasiado,*" Terri said.

"It took many weeks to make," the merchant said. "Is six dollars too much for the work of the three women, day after day, trying to make something that they can sell at a fair price to put bread on the table for their starving children?"

"I'll give you four," Terri said. She was annoyed at herself for her lapse into English. She spoke fourteen languages, and she did not like some Spanish merchant bandit conning her out of a language she used as well as her own.

The merchant shook his head and turned his back to walk away.

That was part of the mercantile courting dance too. Terri put down the shawl she had been looking at and began to inspect a row of shirts hanging randomly from a pipe rack.

The scene was being watched by a man in a tan poplin suit. He looked around and saw that he was, in turn, being watched by a street urchin.

The young boy was physically small, but he had the wary untrusting eyes of an adult who had lived many years.

The man in the poplin suit called him over and when the boy dutifully stood in front of him, the man leaned over to whisper in his ear. The boy listened, then nodded brightly. His eyes lit up with pleasure, and the pleasure was redoubled when the man put two dollars into his hand.

"You are a woman without heart," the merchant said in Spanish.

Terri answered in English. "Not without brains though," she said. "Enough brains not to pay six dollars for something worth only a fraction of that. Four dollars."

The merchant sighed. "Five dollars. That is my very last and best price and the memory of those starving children will be on your head, not mine."

"Sold," Terri said. "But you must promise never to reveal to my friends the outrageous price I paid for this or they will begin to doubt my sanity."

"I'll wrap it," the merchant said. "Although even the price of the wrapping paper makes this transaction a loss to me."

He took the shawl to the counter in the center of the store and measured off a piece of paper to wrap it. He seemed intent on making sure he did not use one millimeter more paper than was absolutely necessary.

Meanwhile, Terri reached in her purse. She was watching the merchant and feeling into her purse with her hand, when suddenly the pocketbook was yanked away from her.

She shrieked and turned to see a small boy holding the purse, running toward the front of the tent-topped shop.

She turned to run after him, but then stopped. A big man reached out a big hand and grabbed the little boy's shoulder. The boy stopped as if he had run into a wall. The big man removed the purse from him, then gave him a paternalistic and not unkind rap on the rear end. The boy ran away without looking back.

The big man in the tan poplin suit looked at Terri and smiled and she felt her heartbeat speed up.

The man stepped forward and handed her the purse.

"Yours, I believe." The accent was British.

Terri just gaped, open-mouthed, for a second, at this quintessential man of her dreams. Then, flustered, she said, "Yes. Thank you."

She took the purse, nodded to the man, and turned back to the merchant, who was still measuring the wrapping paper.

"How much are you paying for that shawl?" the Briton asked.

"Five dollars," Terri said.

"Very good. A very fair price for a fine piece of work. Congratulations."

"She stole it from me," the merchant said.

"I know," the Briton laughed. "And tonight, children will be dying of starvation all over Madrid."

The merchant looked down to hide his smile.

It was love at first sight. Terri had never believed in it because it had never happened to her. Until now.

"Thank you," she mumbled to the man.

"Spot of tea when you're done here?" the man said.

Terri nodded dumbly.

"Well, then, I really should have your name, shouldn't I?" the man said.

"Errr, Terri. Terri Pomfret," she said.

"A lovely name for a lovely lady. My name is Neville," said Neville Lord Wissex.

"Bad news, Little Father," Remo said.

"You're still here," Chiun said.

"If you think that's bad, try this," Remo said. "Smitty wants us to go to Hollywood right away. That's where CURE's records wound up. I told him we needed a vacation."

"Never argue with the emperor," Chiun said. "We will go to Hollywood."

"Hold on, you're up to something. That was just too agreeable and too fast."

"We must go where duty call takes us," Chiun said.

"I got it. You think you can con some producer into making your movie about Sinanju, don't you?"

"I really don't wish to discuss this with you, Remo. You are of a very suspicious turn of mind and it is not flattering to you at all."

"I'll fix you. Every producer I see, I'm going to kill on sight," Remo said.

It was the day she would remember all her life, spent with the man she had wanted to be with all her life.

Terri Pomfret found herself wishing she had a

camera so she could record just the way it had gone. Having tea at a small cafe and then strolling along the riverfront. Spending a long, leisurely, wonderful hour inside a historical chapel, looking at seventeenth-century murals and frescoes.

And now here she was, following Neville, sweet, kind, handsome, charming, cultured Neville, up the steps toward his hotel room. How like him the hotel was. Not flashy or gaudy or tacky. A quiet, genteel building, in a quiet corner of the city, elegant, old-world charming.

She put her hand on the small of his back and Wissex stopped on the stairs and looked down into her eyes. His eyes were the brightest blue she had ever seen. Not dark and hard like Remo's but soft and gentle and caring.

"I've always dreamed of a man like you," she said. He smiled, the smile of one neither embarrassed nor patronizing; the smile of a sharer of the heart's deepest emotions. The smile of a man who understood; who would always understand.

As soon as they entered his room, Neville locked the door behind them, and then drew her into a clinch.

She felt his hands around her back, unbuttoning her blouse, as he steered her into the room, toward the bed. The bed seemed to be beckoning her, calling. She felt her heart pound and her breath catch in her throat and she closed her eyes tightly and buried her face in his neck.

"Oh, take me. Take me," she whispered.

Neville Lord Wissex smiled, and said, "I intend to."

And then he pushed her into a large steamer

trunk at the foot of his bed, slammed the lid and locked it.

At first she shouted, then screamed, but the sound was muffled by heavy styrofoam insulation on the inside of the chest.

Wissex walked to the phone in the room, dialed a number, and said:

"That package is ready."

Remo was wondering where Terri was and when a knock came on their hotel room door, he grumbled, "It's about time," and yelled out, "It's open."

A smartly uniformed bellhop opened the door and stepped inside. To Remo, he said, "Pardon, Señor. There is an old gentleman in this room?"

Remo was lying on the couch. Without rising, he jerked his thumb over his shoulder toward where Chiun stood in a corner of the room, looking out the window.

The bellhop approached the old Korean.

"Señor?"

Chiun turned and the bellhop handed forward a small package wrapped in plain brown paper.

"This was left at the desk. I was told to give it to you," the bellboy said.

Chiun took it and nodded his thanks. The bellhop lingered a moment, as if expecting a tip, then turned and left. Chiun inspected the package, turning it over in his hands.

"What is it?" Remo said, raising himself to a half-sitting position.

"I will not know until I open it," Chiun said.

"Then open it."

"Whose package is this?" Chiun asked.

"Yours, I guess."

"You guess? You didn't guess when that vicious little creature barged in here and asked for an old man. You pointed to me. Old? Since when am I an old man?"

"Since you were eighty years old," Remo said.

"That is old?" Chiun said. "Maybe it is old for a turnip, but for a man, it is not old. Never old."

"Why are you getting all bent out of shape?" Remo asked.

"Because I cannot rid your mind of your Western nonsense, no matter how I try," Chiun said. "Are you always going to go through life, thinking people are old, just because they have seen eight full decades?"

"All right, Chiun, you're young," Remo said. "Open the package."

"No, I am not young," said Chiun.

"What are you then? Christ, help me. I want to know so I don't offend you again."

"I am just right," said Chiun.

"Good," said Remo. "Now we've got that squared away. If we ever get a bellhop asking for the just-right man, I'll know right off it's you."

"Don't forget," said Chiun.

"Open the package," Remo pleaded.

Chiun delicately slit the paper with the long nail of his right index finger. Inside was a small box which he opened and took out a golden object.

"What is it?" Remo asked. "It looks like the handle of a knife."

"It is the handle of a knife. It is a challenge. They have the woman."

Remo got up from the sofa. "Who does?" he asked.

Chiun tossed the knife handle across the room to Remo. Remo caught it and examined the engravings on it: a lion, a sheaf of wheat, and a dagger.

"Same crest we saw back at the bullrun," Remo said. "This is them? The House of something or other?"

"The House of Wissex," Chiun said.

"You're sure this means they have the girl?" Remo asked. He turned the knife handle over in his hand, as if by inspecting it closely he might find something more there than just a knife handle.

"Of course they have the woman," Chiun said. "It is the tradition of the challenge. First they take something of value to you, and then they send a knife to challenge you to come and reclaim your property."

"She's just more trouble than she's worth," Remo said. "Let them have her."

"It is not that simple," Chiun said.

"It never is."

"She is our client and her safety is our responsibility. The House of Sinanju cannot walk away from such a challenge."

"I knew she was going to be troublesome," Remo said.

"It is *our* responsibility, but it is *my* challenge," Chiun said. "It is from one assassin to another."

"And what am I, a chicken wing?"

"No. You are an assassin, but this is a challenge from the Master of Wissex to the Master of Sinanju."

"Tough luck," Remo said. "We go together."

Chiun sighed. "You are truly uneducable."

"Probably, but let's go find the girl," Remo said.

* * *

When the long yacht came within sight of the Hamidian coast, the first faint streaks of sun were smearing the gray sky with pink smudge.

From a telephone in the main cabin, Neville Lord Wissex called Moombasa and awoke him in bed.

"I hope this important," Moombasa said thickly.

"It is. This is Wissex. I have the girl."

"Good. Where's the gold?"

"We don't have that yet," said Wissex.

"Why don't you call me back when you find it?" Moombasa said.

"Wait," said Wissex. "There's more."

"What?"

"Those two men who have been guarding her. I'm sure they will be coming here."

"Should I leave the country?" Moombasa said worriedly. "I can easily schedule my triumphant tour as national liberator. Cuba and Russia keep inviting me."

"No," said Wissex. "I'll deal with those two men. I just wanted you to know."

"Where are you now?" Moombasa asked.

"Just off the coast."

"Don't bring the girl here," said Moombasa.

"Why not?"

"If you bring her here, those two are liable to follow. I don't want them here unless they're already in pieces."

"I won't bring her there. I'm taking her to that hill near your border."

"Mesoro? Why there?"

"Because it suits my purposes," Wissex said.

"It's flat and high and they won't be able to sneak up on me."

"I'll send the Revolutionary Commando Brigade or whatever they call themselves to help you."

"Perish forbid, Wissex said. "Just leave it to me. You could help by keeping patrols and army and everybody else out of the area. I don't want my equipment to be hindered by your people marching around."

"Hokay. I want that woman to talk," Moombasa said.

"She will."

"What does she look like?"

"She's attractive but not your type," Wissex said.

"Too bad. Keep in touch," Moombasa said.

Wissex smiled, replacing the phone. Of course she was not Moombasa's type. The woman had an IQ over 70.

Wissex left the cabin and herded Terri, her hands tightly bound behind her, into the back seat of a helicopter, lashed to a takeoff pad on the small ship's bow.

"Where are we going?" she asked.

"To await the arrival of your friends," Wissex said. He smiled at her and she noticed that his blue eyes were cold and unfeeling. The eyes of a killer. She shuddered at his touch as he pushed her roughly into the aircraft.

From the airport, Remo called Smith again but the CURE director had not been able to find out where the girl had vanished to.

"What the hell good are those computers of yours, Smitty, when they can't find anything out?"

"You forget, Remo. I don't have the computers any more. All the records are still missing. That's why I want you to forget that woman and get back here to the States. Get our records back."

"What about the mountain of gold?" Remo asked. "The death of Western civilization as we know it? What about all that?" Remo asked.

"You know now there is no mountain of gold. So all this is is a kidnapping. The mountain of gold might have been more important than our records, but that woman professor isn't. Come back."

"I can't do that," Remo said.

"Why not?"

"Because her safety is my responsibility. Because the House of Sinanju can't walk away from a challenge."

"I don't understand all that tradition business," Smith said.

"That's because you're uneducable, Smitty. You just hold the fort. We'll get there when we get there," Remo said as he hung up.

As he walked away from the phone booth, Remo saw the same spy who had been dogging his footsteps earlier through Bombay Airport.

The short, squat man was now wearing a flamenco dancer's costume. Little puffballs hung from the fringes of his flat-brimmed hat. He stood by the wall next to the phone booth, edging closer to Remo. His satin trousers squeaked as they rubbed against the marble airport wall.

He smiled at Remo as Remo stepped nearer, the smile one gives a stranger he doesn't really wish to talk to.

"Where is the girl?" Remo said.

"Beg pardon, Señor?"

"The girl."

"We Flamenco dancers have many girls," the man said.

"You know the girl I want," Remo said.

The man shrugged. He was still half shrugged when Remo upended him and dragged him by one fat ankle over to the railing of the observation deck.

Remo tossed him over. The fat man hung upside down, suspended only by Remo's grip on his ankle.

"Where have they taken her?" Remo growled.

"Hamidia," the man screamed in terror. "Hamidia. To Mesoro. True. True. I tell the truth, Señor."

"I know you do," Remo said. "Have a nice trip."

He let the man fall and walked away, even before the scream died out with a fat splat. Chiun was standing in front of an arcade filled with electronic games.

"They've gone to Hamidia. Some place named Mesoro," Remo said.

Chiun nodded and said, "Japs are treacherous. I bet we could have played Space Invaders on that other one's machine."

Generalissimo Moombasa didn't like to rise before noon. It was his opinion that in people's democratic republics, anything that happened before noon deserved to wait for the great man to get out of bed.

But the call from Lord Wissex had disrupted his smooth sleeping pattern and he rested only fitfully for two more hours until his private telephone rang again.

If this kept up, he was going to have it disconnected, he decided.

"Hello," he yelled into the phone.

"Ehhhhhhhhhhhhh. This is Pimsy Wissex," a voice rattled.

"Sorry, you got wrong number. You want asthma clinic, you look up number. The house of fancy boys is down the street too. You look up their number."

He hung up the telephone but it rang again instantly.

"What now?"

"Listen to me, you bleeding wog," Pimsy snarled. "I've got something to tell you."

"This better be important."

"It is," said Uncle Pimsy.

Seventeen

Night was falling. She had hung there through the brutally hot sun of the day with not a drop of water for her lips. Her arms felt that they were going to snap out of her shoulder sockets and twice during the day when she could stand the pain no more, she had screamed and Wissex had lowered her to the ground for fifteen minutes before hoisting her up again.

Her throat was parched and her lips were dry. She touched them with her tongue but it felt like rubbing wood over wood.

At least the night would bring some coolness, some relief from the day's heat. But in the grassy fields below that surrounded the flat-topped hill they were on, Terri could hear the insects and then the sounds of larger animals—a snarl, a growl—and the thought of what was out there chilled her.

She was hanging from a long boom, extended out over the edge of the Mesoro Hill. Ropes tied roughly around her wrists were fastened to the boom, and she was able to rest only by grabbing the boom with her hands and holding on, to rest her wrists, until her hands tired of supporting her weight and she had to let go. And then the pain in the wrists began again.

The boom was attached at its other end to a heavy, complicated tripod in the center of the flat table of rock. And Lord Wissex sat there, at a table which he had unloaded from the helicopter, a table with controls built into it. During the heat of the day, he had opened a bottle of white wine which he had carried in a cooler, had poured himself a glass, and had toasted Terri Pomfret's beauty.

But he had offered her none for her dry throat.

He was a sadist and a brute. She had fallen for the accent and the superficial charm and the tweedy British clothes and she realized that if Jack the Ripper had ben been soft-spoken and full of "yes, m'dears" and worn an ascot, she probably would have crawled into a blood-stained bed with him.

She saw Wissex looking at her and she asked again, "What are you going to do with me?" He had not answered her all day when she had asked that question.

Wissex smiled at her. "Do you know that that imbecile Moombasa still believes there is a mountain of gold?" he asked.

"And there isn't," she said.

"Of course not," Wissex said.

"Why did you put up all those plaques? It was you, wasn't it?"

"Of course m'dear. It was my plan. There is, you know, this idiotic Hamidian legend about a mountain of gold. It was my idea that if I got Moombasa to believe the United States was looking for it, then he would spend any amount of money to find it. So far, he has been good for twenty million dollars."

"He's not going to be happy when he finds out there's no mountain," Terri said.

"He thinks there is one. He thinks you'll tell him where it is."

"It doesn't exist," Terri said. "I'll tell him that. And that it was all your idea."

Wissex chuckled. "I know that and you know that. But I'm afraid you won't get a chance to tell him. Unfortunately, m'dear, you're going to have an accident. A fatal accident."

"But why the plaques?" she asked again.

"That was to lend authenticity to the scheme," he said. "You should realize that true genius involves painstaking attention to detail. I wanted everything to look correct. It had to be good enough not only to fool Moombasa—I could fool him with a map drawn in the sand with a stick—but also to fool you and the United States until I extracted enough money from that idiot. He is not a trusting sort. Did you know that he has had one of his would-be spies traipsing around, trying to keep an eye on you and your bodyguards?"

"That fat man at the airport?" Terri said.

"Yes. I made sure to tell him where we were going. I have no doubt that your friends have, by now, extracted that information from him."

Terri felt her heart add a little extra happy beat. "But why?" she asked him and because she guessed it would feed his macho sense of himself, she added, "I don't understand. Why would you want them to know where we went?"

"Because I am going to kill them. Those two

have spoiled my calculations long enough and they have been a shadow over the House of Wissex for far too many years. When they come for you, all three of you will die."

He spoke with an unemotional flatness as if he were discussing the score of last year's semifinal soccer game.

"They'll get you, you know," Terri said, the anger spilling out of her, fueled by his smugness. "They're better than you are."

"Don't you believe it, girl. Don't you believe it. And now I wish you would please be still. I have some cogitation to do to prepare my welcome for the House of Sinanju."

"Still? I won't be still. I'll shout and scream and let the world know I'm here." Terri opened her mouth to scream, but it changed to a shriek of pain as Wissex pressed a button on the panel in front of him and the boom yanked her upwards, almost dislocating her arms from her shoulders. She bit her lip and hung there in silence, looking across at him, at the helicopter parked on the hilltop behind him. Wissex must have set a trap for Remo and Chiun—but what could it be? She would not let them die, not if she could help it. When she saw them, she would shout and scream and let them know it was a trap. And if she died, then maybe she deserved it for being stupid, but at least she would have evened the score with this English monster.

But while the night grew darker, her resolve and her courage weakened, as the night sounds surrounding the hilltop grew in intensity. She tried to spin on her ropes, to look around her in a full

360-degree circle, to see if she could see a light that might be Remo and Chiun, but even as she made the effort, she heard Wissex' mocking voice.

"Don't trouble yourself. When they arrive, I will let you know. Nothing can move out there without being detected by my sensors. That is why we came to this godforsaken lump of dirt. It is the only high ground in this entire country and I will know they are coming long before they get here. So just hang there and rest." He laughed again and Terri felt her heart sink.

There was just no hope, no chance for survival, no way to save Remo and Chiun from this evil madman.

"Oh, that's awful," Remo said. He was looking up at Terri, perilously extended from the boom out over the edge of the hill. "That bastard."

He dropped back to the ground alongside Chiun.

"Do you feel it?" Remo hissed.

"Of course," Chiun said softly.

"It's some kind of force field," Remo said. "Probably a detection device to tell him we're here."

"I know what it is, you untrained monkey," Chiun said.

"How do we avoid it? That's the problem."

"There was once a Master Yung Suk," Chiun started but Remo interrupted.

"Now you're going to give me a history lesson? Now?"

"There are no new answers; only new questions," Chiun said.

"What's that supposed to mean?" asked Remo.

"It means that there was once a Master Yung Suk," Chiun said.

"Can we keep this one short before Terri dies hanging up there?"

"And Yung Suk was supposed to storm the castle of an evil prince. This was in Mongolia. Don't worry about the girl; I noticed she has very strong arms. And the evil prince knew an attack was coming and he had all his best soldiers atop his castle, along the walls, looking off in all four directions. And the prince had his spies about too and the spies found that the attack would come from Yung Suk and four of the best men of the village. So when five men came out of the woods surrounding the castle, a great cry and shout went up from the soldiers and they attacked and overwhelmed the five men and killed them."

"That's some freaking cheery wonderful story," Remo said.

"It is not over."

"What else?" Remo asked.

"And while the soldiers were laying waste these five, Master Yung Suk entered the castle from the other side and killed the evil prince and got paid and everything ended happily."

"What's the moral?" asked Remo.

"The moral is that armies and Englishmen see only what they have been warned that they might see. This Wissex upstart up there is expecting two. We will give him two and he will concentrate on two and then there will be a third and that will do the trick," Chiun said.

"There's only two of us. How are we going to be three?"

Chiun stood up and stepped back into the darkness a few yards. Remo heard a soft wrenching sound as if a grave were giving up its cargo. A moment later, Chiun was back, his arms wrapped around a small eight-foot-high tree. He tossed the tree toward Remo.

"I get it," Remo said. "We use the tree to divert him and make him think it's one of us."

"At last the dawn," Chiun said. "Even after the darkest night."

"You want me to go with the tree?" Remo said. "How about you?"

"You already clomp around with enough noise for two," Chiun said. "You are much more believable imitating a crowd."

"Okay."

Chiun pointed Remo off toward the left side of the hill, and as the old man watched, Remo moved away into the darkness, lugging the tree, as silent as a wisp of air. When he knew that Remo could not see him, Chiun nodded his head approvingly. Some never learned to move. There had even been masters who were lead-footed; but Remo had learned in the earliest days of his training to center his weight, so he could move smoothly in any direction. One of the fairy tales Chiun had been told as a child was the story of a master who could run across a wet field and leave not a crushed blade of grass behind him. When he was growing up in his training, Chiun thought it impossible, a fairy tale, but now he thought that someday Remo might be able to do it. Perhaps even better than Chiun himself.

Chiun listened but heard nothing except the

sounds of the night. No movement from Remo, not even the hiss of a breath, not even the rustling of a leaf on the small tree the young American carried.

And then Chiun drifted off toward the right side of the hill, above which hung the terrified form of Terri Pomfret.

"Here they come," Wissex said softly.

It was fully dark now and from Terri's point of view, Wissex's face was distorted in the green flickering light of a television monitor built into the table before him. The green light threw long fright shadows up across Wissex's face. Terri wondered how she had ever thought he was handsome.

Wissex looked at the screen and laughed softly at their crude attempt to deceive him. The screen was built into a television but it was the latest form of radar screen, picking up the movement of objects over the size of a child.

Four overlapping cameras that Wissex had mounted on the edges of the tabletop mesa scanned the area around the hill.

Wissex watched the movement of the two men on the screen. First one of them would dart forward, fifteen feet or so, close to the edge of the camera's range. Then the other would move forward, and join with the first. Then the first would move forward again. It was obvious to Wissex that they were trying to find a pocket of space that the cameras didn't cover.

Not a chance, he thought. He reached under the table and opened a small case from which he took a submachine gun. He clicked off its safety and set the first round into the chamber, then waited, his eyes watching the screen, as the two figures continued their unusual leapfrog motion toward the base of the hill. Only forty yards more and they would be at the bottom of the cliff.

They would have to climb up. And he would be waiting.

Remo tossed the tree forward fifteen feet and waited until it hit. Then he ran forward himself until he was on a line with the tree, then turned sharply to his right and moved over to the tree. He waited a few seconds, then tossed the tree forward again and repeated the maneuver.

Chiun should be at the base of the hill now, Remo thought.

Terri saw him as the moon came out from behind a cloud for a brief moment. It flashed on the dark purple of the kimono and she saw Chiun's face, looking upward, as he came silently up the stone face of the hill. She had been looking at that wall all day and it had been smooth and seemed impossible to scale, but Chiun was moving upward as rapidly as if he had been climbing a ladder.

She glanced over toward Wissex at the platform in the center of the hill but he had seen nothing. His eyes were still riveted on the television screen.

And Chiun was climbing.

Remo had reached the bottom of the hill. He dropped the tree and looked up at the smooth stone walls. If he went up, Wissex had only to look over the edge and he could pick Remo off like a wingless fly clinging to a wall.

He hoped Chiun's scheme was working and the Briton was still focusing his attention on Remo. Maybe . . . if he kept that attention.

Remo backed off from the wall and shouted out.

"Wissex, we're here for you. Surrender the girl."

He waited a split second, then got his answer, a deep, rolling laugh that shattered the quiet of the night.

And then Wissex's voice.

"Come on up. I'm waiting for you. You can join the wench."

She saw Chiun put a hand over the top of the cliff and then, like smoke rising, he moved up onto the edge. Wissex had moved to the other side of the hill, from the bottom of which had come Remo's voice. His back was to Chiun but the old man did not move. He had his head cocked as if listening to something far off.

Suddenly, Terri heard it too.

It was a distant rumbling, like the sound of machinery.

Wissex heard it too and spun toward the noise and he saw Chiun. Even as he said, in confusion, "How . . . what are you doing here?" he aimed the spray machine gun in Chiun's direction.

The Korean did not answer.

"There are three of you?" Wissex said.

"Perhaps four or five," Chiun said.

"It doesn't matter," Wissex said. "However many there are, they are all dead."

The sound came from trucks. Terri could recognize the noise now. And then the sound lessened, and search lights flamed from out of the darkness toward the hill. Then a voice boomed through the night, powerful amplification making it seem that it came from every direction at once.

"Wissex, I know all," shouted Moombasa. "And now you die, thieving Englishman."

"That damned wog," Wissex said. "I'm getting out of here." He raised the gun toward Chiun. "But first you."

Remo had lingered at the base of the hill but when he heard the first machine gun blast, he leaped upward, grabbed a finger hold and began to move up the face of the smooth rock. It had been the hardest of lessons when he was young in Sinanju, learning to put the pressure of his weight into the face of the wall he was climbing and not down toward the ground. Harder still to learn was to harness the fear of falling that brought tension to the muscles and made the act of climbing impossible.

There was another burst from the machine gun and Remo raced toward the top of the cliff.

Moombasa heard the machine-gun fire too and he ducked down inside the 1948 Studebaker that was the pride of Hamidia's armored corps. He dropped his megaphone on his driver's head.

"That limey is trying to harm my royal person," he said. "Attack," he shouted. "Attack. Reduce that hill to rubble. I don't want a stone left."

His driver moved the Studebaker out of the way of the seven cannons, mounted on the backs of flatbed trucks, as uniformed soldiers loaded the big guns and began sighting in on the flat mountain top.

Even though she had seen it, she didn't believe it. Terri had seen Wissex aim the gun at Chiun and press the trigger. The old man hadn't seemed to move and yet somehow the bullets had missed and Chiun was ten feet away from his previous position. Then he circled slowly away from Wissex and Terri realized that he was turning Wissex away from her, to protect her from being hit by a stray shot.

Wissex wheeled toward Chiun. He held the machine gun at waist level and then squeezed the trigger again, this time letting out a spray of bullets in a wide arc. And again, they missed, because when Wissex released the trigger, the old man was still standing, still smiling, and then he moved forward toward Wissex.

"My ancestor let yours live," Chiun intoned. "You will not be so lucky. This is the last time you pretenders attack the House of Sinanju."

Wissex looked at Chiun and the gun, then threw the gun on the ground and bolted toward the helicopter on the far side of the mesa.

He got only two steps before being hauled up short. Terri saw him. It was Remo, moving out of the night, wearing his regular black chinos and black t-shirt, and he had his hand on Wissex's shoulder.

Wissex wheeled to face him.

"No, no, no," he cried. "My challenge was not to you, American. It was to Sinanju."

"And I am the next Master of Sinanju," Remo said.

Terri saw Wissex' face pale. Then he pulled away from Remo and tried to run but again Remo stopped him with a hand on his shoulder.

Terri saw Remo flick a finger toward Wissex' neck. Wissex reached up to touch his throat.

"What was that?" he asked. "I hardly felt it."

"Don't turn your head," Remo said.

"Why not?" asked Wissex.

He turned his head.

And as Terri looked on, his head fell off.

Remo looked down at the body and said, "That's the biz, sweetheart."

He ran over toward Terri. "You all right?"

"Just arm weary," she said. "Get me down from here."

"Coming right up," Remo said.

He scampered up onto the long boom and walked out along it to where Terri was hanging. She looked up between her hands and saw him break the ropes between his fingers, and then take her hands in his. Easily, he lifted her and walked back along the boom until they were both over the safe rock of the hilltop. Then he set her down carefully.

Chiun came over to look at the girls' wrists in the illumination from the floodlights on the trucks below. He began to massage them gently.

"Too much thumb," he said to Remo.

"What?"

Chiun nodded toward Wissex' body. "With him," he said. "Too much thumb on that stroke."

"It needed thumb," Remo said.

"You are a disrespectful galoot," Chiun said.

This was a new word he had learned only a few weeks before watching a cowboy movie and he was practicing using it on Remo. "Yes," he said. "Heh, heh. Just a galoot."

Suddenly, they heard the whistle of an approaching shell, and then felt a shudder as the shell hit and exploded near the mountain's base. Then they heard Moombasa's voice, shouting out over the loudspeaker.

"Fire. Destroy the British devil. Level that mountain. Not a stone left."

"We'd better get out of here before they get the range," Terri said.

"That probably gives us till next month," Remo said.

Chiun pointed toward the helicopter. "There is that whirly thing. Can you fly it?"

"If it's got wings, I can fly it," Remo said.

"Actually, it does not have wings," Chiun said.

"Actually, I can't fly it," said Remo.

"I can," Terri said.

"Thank God for liberated women," Remo said.

The shell bombardment was slowly getting closer and as the three clambered into the helicopter, a shell exploded only 20 yards from them on the hilltop.

Quickly and competently, Terri started the helicopter's motor and turned on the craft's lights. She looked outside at the hill, then jumped from the pilot's seat and ran back onto the hilltop.

"Remo, Chiun. Come quick," she called.

When they got to her, she was kneeling over the shell hole. At the bottom of the hole, the ground was glittering. Chiun reached in and pulled out a small pellet.

"Gold," he said.

"It's the mountain! The gold mountain. This is it. Yahooooo," Terri yelled.

They heard the whistle of another shell. It hit only 25 feet away and the concussion of the explosion pitched Terri onto her back.

She scrambled to her feet and shook her fist in Moombasa's direction.

"It's the gold mountain, you imbecile!"

From his vantage point below, Moombasa saw only a figure on the edge of the hill shaking a fist at him.

He picked up his loudspeaker and bellowed, "Taunt me, Englishman? We will destroy you. Fire. Fire. Fire. Bury that hill in the dirt."

Remo and Chiun helped Terri Pomfret back into the helicopter and she lifted the craft. It hovered for a moment, and then swooped down along the far side of the mountain, out of sight of Moombasa's artillery.

"The idiot's going to bury the hill," Remo said.

"Good. Then he'll never know the gold was there."

"And maybe our guys can sneak in some time and take it out and nobody'll be the wiser."

Chiun was silent and Remo asked him, "Something on your mind, Little Father?"

"Yes."

"What?"

"The House of Sinanju owes an apology."

"To whom?" asked Remo.

"To Puk. No more can he be called Puk the Liar. He told the truth."

"Good old Puk," said Remo.

"You know what must have happened?" Terri said. She was flying the copter low now, barely skimming tree tops, on her way toward the ocean. "When the Spanish came, the Hamidians brought their gold out here and built that hill around it. Then they told the Spanish that the gold had been sent all over the world. And nobody ever knew. The Spanish massacred the Hamidians and the secret died with them. It's been sitting here all that time."

"Until now," Remo said. "When that nutcake is done, it won't even be a smear."

"Maybe it's best," Terri said. "Let the Hamidian legend die with them."

"I guess so," Remo said.

"It's a lot of gold," Chiun said.

Eighteen

Sometimes things just seemed to work right, even when they started out wrong.

That thought occurred to Barry Schweid, after he received the telephone call from the mysterious producer, Mr. Smith, to meet him right away at the offices of Universal Bindle Marmelstein Mammoth Global Magnificent Productions Inc.

But when Barry went outside, all four tires were flat on his 1971 Volkswagen.

But the bad luck turned good right away because, just by chance, there was a cab parked in front of his house.

The cabbie was a dark-haired young man who didn't talk much. From the back seat, Schweid noticed that the driver had very thick wrists.

He also noticed that the driver didn't seem to know his way around Los Angeles too well, because he couldn't ever seen to find Wilshire Boulevard.

"Can't you get me there?" Barry Schweid said. "This is an important meeting."

"Don't worry," the driver said. "He'll wait."

* * *

Inside Barry Schweid's home, Dr. Harold W. Smith had the telephone hookup in place. He had learned a lesson from the last fiasco of trying to move CURE's records to St. Martin Island. Never again would he put all his eggs in one basket.

He listened over the telephone for the signals that indicated both receivers were ready.

Then he pressed the transmit switches on Schweid's word processor computer, and listened as the tapes began to whir.

It took seventeen minutes for all CURE's records to be transmitted across telephone lines to St. Martin. *And* back to CURE headquarters at Folcroft. From here on in, CURE would maintain double files.

As the computer continued to whir, Smith allowed himself a small smile. CURE was still operating; the battle against America's enemies had not yet been lost.

Twenty-seven minutes later, the taxicab pulled up to the curb.

Schweid looked out the window and squawked, "Hey. This is my house again. What are you doing?"

The driver ignored him. He rolled down the front passenger window and called out: "Got him, Smitty."

As Schweid watched, a thin man in a three-piece gray suit stepped from the bushes alongside his front entrance, walked quickly to the taxi, and got into the backseat alongside Schweid.

"You want me to drive, Smitty?" the cabby said.

"No. Just stay here." The gray-suited man turned to Schweid. "I'm Mr. Smith."

"Well, I'm really glad to——" But before he could extend his hand, Schweid was cut off by Smith.

"You should know this," Smith said. "Bindle and Marmelstein are planning to steal your screenplay. They've already tried to sell it to me."

"My assassin movie?" asked Schweid.

"Right," Smith said. "According to them, they've got it tied up tight."

"I'll burn it before I let it be stolen," Schweid said.

"That's just what I want you to do," Smith said. "I want you to go inside your house and erase that screenplay from your computer. Wipe the tapes clean. And there'll be a check for you in the mail tomorrow."

"I knew it was too good to be true," Schweid said. "I just knew that movie would never be made. I'm going to destroy the screenplay right now. And all that other stuff I've got in my machine."

"Good," said Smith.

Schweid started out of the cab. "It didn't have a chance," he said. "I knew that."

The cabdriver said, "What do you mean? It didn't have a chance?"

"It was just too farfetched and too unbelievable," Schweid said. "A superkiller working for the government. No one would buy that."

"I guess you're right," said Remo Williams as Schweid left the cab and walked toward his house.

After he had gone inside, Remo turned around from the driver's seat and said to Smith, "Suppose he doesn't wipe his tapes clean?"

"It doesn't matter," Smith said. "I already did. There's nothing left on them. And he just didn't have any idea of what the information was. He's harmless."

"Good," said Remo. "Where to?"

"Let's go see Bindle and Marmelstein," Smith said.

Hank Bindle and Bruce Marmelstein smiled in unison as Mr. Smith walked into the office, followed by a dark-haired young man in a black t-shirt and chinos.

"Mr. Smith, I presume," said Marmelstein, extending a hand in greeting.

"I want Schweid's screenplays," Smith said coldly.

"Which one?" said Marmelstein.

"All of them."

"You're going to produce them all?" asked Bindle.

"Yes," said Smith. "I want my creative people to read them over first. Then the three of us will have a meeting to discuss them. And the price."

"Okay," said Marmelstein. "We'll give a meeting." He pointed to Remo. "Who's he?"

"He's my creative people," said Smith. "Do something creative."

Remo creatively broke Marmelstein's marble desk top in half.

The two partners handed Smith a packet of screenplays.

"They're all in here," Bindle said. "Every one of them."

Smith glanced through them to make sure the one he wanted was there. He saw the title: *Loves of an Assassin*.

"Did you two read these?" Smith asked.

"Actually, no," said Bindle.

"Why not?" asked Smith.

"Actually, we don't read," said Marmelstein.

"Good," said Remo. "Then actually you don't die."

Smith turned toward the door and Remo followed him.

Bindle called out: "Mr. Smith. When you see that *Hamlet* script, you're going to love it. And we can do it for you. Every step of the way. We can give you the greatest *Hamlet* of all time."

"With tits," said Marmelstein.